P9-DMP-536

Annie's Attic
Mysteries™

THE Lady IN THE Attic

TARA RANDEL

Annie's®
AnniesFiction.com

Books in the Annie's Attic Mysteries series

The Lady in the Attic
Copyright © 2021 Annie's.

All rights reserved. No part of this publication may be reproduced, stored in a retrieval system, or transmitted in any form or by any means—electronic, mechanical, photocopying, recording or otherwise—without the prior written permission of the publisher. The only exception is brief quotations in printed reviews. For information address Annie's, 306 East Parr Road, Berne, Indiana 46711-1138.

The characters and events in this book are fictional, and any resemblance to actual persons or events is coincidental.

Library of Congress-in-Publication Data
Lady in the Attic / by Tara Randel
p. cm.
I. Title
                    2021936157

AnniesFiction.com
800-282-6643
Annie's Attic Mysteries ®
Series Editors: Janice Tate and Ken Tate
Series Creator: Stenhouse & Associates, Ridgefield, Connecticut

10 11 12 13 14 | Printed in China | 9 8 7 6 5 4 3 2

─ Prologue ─

Mom, we're fine. We don't need you here any longer. The story of her life, Annie Dawson thought as her daughter's words replayed over and over in her mind. LeeAnn had recently undergone a minor surgical procedure, and Annie had gladly helped out while her daughter recovered. It hadn't been serious, but LeeAnn had needed a few days off her feet. Taking care of her five-year-old twin grandchildren—John and Joanna—had required a lot of work, but Annie had loved it. The days had flown by until LeeAnn decided to send Annie on her way, saying she was ready to get back to the task of taking care of her family.

Now at loose ends, Annie glanced down at the yarn twined around her hook. This was the third blanket she'd crocheted for a church baby shower this year. Ever since her husband, Wayne, had passed away last year, she'd been aimless, and with LeeAnn capable of taking care of herself, where did she fit in now?

She sighed deeply, laying the baby blanket on her lap to stare out over her front yard. The late Texas spring had turned the grass to a gentle green. Wildflowers in rich hues of blue, yellow, and pink bloomed in profusion along the fence near the main road. Before long, the temperature would shoot from pleasurable to just darn hot. Another spring would lead to another summer, autumn ... and a new year. Another year spent rambling around the big house with only herself for company. Shaking her head, she glanced down at the nearly finished stroller blanket of squares and rectangles with heart motifs in varying shades of pink outlined with white. She picked up the hook and soft yarn, returning to the task at hand. She was just finishing a row when the phone rang.

"Should have brought the handset outside," she muttered as she hurried indoors to answer before the answering machine clicked on. Breathless, she answered, "Hello."

"Mrs. Dawson? My name is Gordon Procter. I'm the attorney for your late grandmother, Elizabeth Holden."

The ache of sadness that had only just started to diminish filled her again. Two weeks ago Gram had passed on, filling Annie with about as much heartache as she could handle. When she first received the news, she couldn't believe it. Granted, Gram had been in her late eighties and it was probably her time, but Annie's memories were of a vital, active woman. She couldn't wrap her mind around the fact that Gram would no longer be there for advice or just to chat.

"How can I help you?"

"I'm calling to inform you that your grandmother left you Grey Gables and all its contents."

Annie paused, surprised. "She left me the house?" Even though her parents had died—her mother, five years ago from tuberculosis contracted in Africa, her dad, two years later from a stroke—it never crossed Annie's mind that she would inherit everything.

"Yes. I'll need to have you sign off on the property and

straighten out a few other particulars of her will. Can you take care of these details?"

"If that's what Gram wanted, of course."

"Excellent. Then I'll see you when you arrive in Stony Point."

"Wait. Say that again?"

"Stony Point. Maine. Where Grey Gables is located."

"Well, yes, I know where that is. Can't we do this over the phone?"

"Mrs. Dawson, you'll need to make some decisions about the house. There is paperwork involved, so coming here makes perfect sense." He must have sensed her trepidation because he quickly added, "Why don't you think about this? I can handle it all for you if you wish."

"Yes, I'll think about it and get back to you. Thanks." She returned the phone to its cradle.

Gram had left her Grey Gables?

Annie wandered back out to the porch, her mind spinning just as it had when the doctor had called with the news of Gram passing away in her sleep. Thankfully, she hadn't suffered. But the call had come on the same day as LeeAnn's surgery. Torn by the dilemma Annie found herself in, she knew she'd never make it in time for the funeral, so she elected to stay with her grandchildren. She knew that Gram would understand.

How many years had it been since she'd been to Maine? Not since before her daughter, LeeAnn, had been born. With a new baby and the Dawson car dealership to run with Wayne, there hadn't been time for her summer trips back east, so Annie had always flown Gram to Dallas, picking her up at the airport and driving her home to Brookfield.

Yet after all the years away, she still remembered those childhood trips with pleasure. Her parents sent her to stay with Gram while they went on their first missionary trip. After that first summer, there was no question about her returning. Every year when school ended, Annie would pack her bags and spend an idyllic summer with Gram. She'd scoured every inch of Grey Gables, a Victorian house on the edge of the town of Stony Point. She'd also investigated every inch of the property and then some. Those summers had been special, as had been Gram—her confidante and best friend for as long as Annie could remember.

But travel more than two thousand miles to settle her grandmother's affairs?

On the other hand, how could she not go if Gram had entrusted the house to her? The thought of strangers disposing of the contents or actually selling the grand old place before seeing it one last time didn't sit well.

She grabbed the blanket and placed it in the nearby basket, carrying it inside as she hurried into the den to find an atlas. Brookfield to Stony Point would be quite a journey. Yet something she'd missed since Wayne died last year, something she couldn't quite put her finger on, tingled in her. The thought of going back to her childhood haunt enveloped her heart in warmth. She found herself considering the idea, actually looking forward to seeing the place, even though it wouldn't be the same without Gram there.

Sinking down into the desk chair, she gazed at a picture of Wayne and her, taken a few years ago—so happy and carefree. How handsome he was, his dark brown hair combed neatly, laugh lines radiating from his deep blue eyes, his ready smile. Her blond hair, much longer in the picture and without the new gray, had since been cut shorter. Her green eyes had lost their sparkle, especially after all the trauma of the past year.

She missed Wayne, plain and simple. They'd talked about traveling more than their usual weekend get-away after LeeAnn married and happily settled into her life, but the demands of the Chevy dealership had kept Wayne busy. Soon the days turned to years, and they rarely left Brookfield for a real vacation. Since Wayne's death, she'd sold the dealership, unable to face the day-to-day demands of running it without her husband at her side. Now she was free to come and go as she pleased. Yet she hadn't done a thing. Gone was the excitement and color in her life. She reached for a recent photo of LeeAnn's family and gazed longingly at the happy faces.

And as much as she loved LeeAnn and the grandchildren and tried to spend plenty of time with them, they couldn't fill the void that had become her life. She'd raised LeeAnn to be self-sufficient. It had certainly worked; LeeAnn didn't need her as much as Annie would have liked. With all the changes and loss in the past year, Annie had lost her sense of place—of purpose.

Maybe now she had a chance to do something about it. All because of Gram.

A road trip, that's what she needed. Wayne had insisted she keep her car, a Malibu, in good shape, even with the high mileage. It was one of the perks of having owned a dealership. She could have traded it in but loved scooting around town in the sporty car. Now, she had a chance to drive cross-country and see a bit of the States before dealing with Grey Gables.

Could she do this?

Did she want to do this?

All by herself?

She rose and crossed to the window, staring up at the vast blue sky. If she decided to go, she'd spend her first summer in nearly thirty years back in Maine.

A bubble of laughter escaped her. She was really going to do this.

Turning, she went back to the desk, snatched up the phone handset, and with shaking fingers punched in her daughter's telephone number. "LeeAnn, you aren't going to believe this ..."

~ 1 ~

Annie turned off the ignition of her old Malibu and gazed up at the stately white Victorian house. Grey Gables.

She'd made it.

The trip had taken a week. Annie hadn't rushed, making the drive at a steady clip, but not overdoing it. And now she was here, staring out at her childhood memories.

With a gusty sigh, she exited the car, inhaling the fresh scent of salty air and early summer sunshine. Walking a few feet, she stopped at the raggedy edge of grass spilling onto the walkway.

Everything looked much the same. An amazing open porch traversed the front of the house, allowing a spectacular view of the nearby ocean. Tall pillars supported a wide roof over the porch, featuring a graceful arch over the stairs. A tattered screen door welcomed the weary traveler to come in and rest.

Annie frowned. *Tattered?* She narrowed her eyes, really seeing the house before her without the shiny patina of her memories coloring her view.

The house paint, blistered and peeling, sported grime on the once-neat trim. The large, long windows wore years of dust. A few weathered floorboards on the wide steps warped upward.

Annie tentatively made her way up the steps onto the porch. The wood flooring had lost its luster to the elements. How long had Grey Gables been in such a sorry state? She remembered brightness. Now everything seemed dull.

Except for the view. White-tipped waves undulating over the deep blue of the ocean. Heavy rocks hugging the shoreline. Breathtaking. Especially seen through the eyes of an adult, not the carefree child who had explored this rugged terrain and taken it for granted. And she was grateful that someone had planted an array of impatiens among the shrubs all across the front.

Digging into her purse, she removed the key she'd picked up at Mr. Procter's office early that afternoon. She'd been tired from the trip, so she set up an appointment to go over the estate tomorrow morning. With key in hand, she'd stopped by Hansen's Gas N Go to buy a few staples, and then drove the short distance from town, to her destination.

Only this wasn't what she expected. Chilled, even though the temperature hovered near a pleasant seventy-five degrees, she unlocked the door, unease washing over her as she stepped over the threshold.

She expected the scent of potpourri to greet her, not the lingering closed-in musty odor. Gram had always made her own potpourri, enlisting Annie's help whenever she visited. Today, however, Annie only noticed the scent of neglect.

Just inside the door, an artfully framed cross-stitch her grandmother had stitched years ago still hung on the wall. It was Gram's first originally designed piece that had introduced her to craft circles, the only one she'd never sold or gifted. Friends had urged her to enter her projects in local craft shows. Through the years, her unique designs featuring countryside scenes drew critical acclaim, and Gram's fame grew. Craft books and magazines featured her original patterns. She founded a cross-stitch society that spread throughout New England. Nowadays, a Betsy Original was a collector's item. Annie knew this; she had a beautifully stitched meadow scene hanging in her living room back home.

In her mind's eye, she pictured her grandmother laboring over custom designs—and the pride on her face upon finishing a piece. Annie teased Gram about being a celebrity, but the modest woman blushed and never put on airs.

After gazing at the cross-stitch for a long minute, Annie wandered down the hallway. To the left lay the living room, filled with overstuffed furniture covered in a floral print. To the right, the grand and fancy dining room featured a heavy mahogany table and china cabinet. She continued down the hall, stopping to poke her head into the small library. Volume after volume of books lined the shelves. Annie loved this room, having curled up on the window seat more than once to be swept away in the pages of *Little Women* or *The Black Stallion*. Gram would join her, sitting in her comfy chair and working on a project, whether crocheting or cross-stitching. In fact, Gram had given Annie her first crochet hook and a ball of yarn in this very room, teaching a young girl her very first chain stitches.

Finally, at the back of the house, she entered the large, homey kitchen. She and Gram had spent most of their time here, cooking meals, baking fresh fruit pies, or just talking. Annie knew it was wishful thinking on her part, but she could have sworn she smelled Gram's famous peach cobbler in the air.

After her tour of the first floor, Annie threw the windows open wide, welcoming the fresh, clean sea breeze. In the kitchen, she opened the door, stepping out onto the flagstone patio. Gram had stood here many times, calling Annie home for a meal when she'd been out exploring, most of the time in places Gram warned her against. Yet another lovely view greeted her—a sprawling backyard. Wild azaleas bordered one side, black-eyed Susans and myriad purple, pink, and white wildflowers overtook the other side, opening to the entrance path leading down to the rocky shoreline. Gram had loved her flowers as much as her needlework. "Must have been where I got it," Annie whispered.

Once the house was open, Annie ventured back out to the car to get her luggage. She'd made her third, and final, trip to the house when she noticed a woman walking up the driveway. Annie stopped, shaded her eyes, and waited for the woman to approach. Could this be the Stony Point welcoming committee?

"Hello, there, Annie," came the flat-accented greeting. The slim woman, with auburn hair and striking blue eyes, held a gray cat with white feet. Interesting. As she moved closer, Annie determined that they might be about the same age, give or take a wrinkle or two.

Wait. Could it be? "Alice?"

"I'm surprised you remember me," the woman said, her tone frosty. "We never did see each other after your last summer here. That was decades ago."

"For which I take full responsibility," Annie said, trying

for a little levity. "You know how life just happens."

"I suppose," she said with a humph.

"And here I was, ready to remind you about the time we climbed the tallest apple tree in Smith's orchard and got stuck. Gram called the fire department to get us down, and it seemed like the whole town, including Tommy Jenkins, who we both had a crush on, didn't let us live it down all summer."

A small smile played over Alice's lips.

Despite the less-than-stellar greeting, Annie ran over to hug her old friend. "My goodness. Has it really been that long?"

"I hate to admit it, but yes. You never kept in touch. I had to hear about you from your grandmother." Alice stepped back to view Annie, her expression marginally warmer. "I was sorry to hear about your husband."

"Thanks."

Alice paused, her tone wary. "You look great."

"So do you." In fact, Alice was stunning. A far cry from the skinny girl Annie remembered. "How did you know I was here?"

"I saw the car pull in the driveway and knew it had to be you. I can't imagine your grandmother leaving the grand old place to anyone else."

Annie squinted at the house. "Grand? I'm not so sure."

"You missed the funeral," Alice blurted, censure heavy in her words.

"And I'm so sorry I did." Annie explained about taking care of her grandchildren.

"I helped to take care of the arrangements."

"I appreciate it." A knot formed in Annie's throat. "I wish I could have come."

An awkward silence fell between them, until the cat meowed and squirmed in earnest. Alice let out a yelp, and the animal flew out of her arms. "That would be Boots," she pointed out as the cat flew up the steps and disappeared into the house.

"One of Gram's strays?"

"The last one."

Annie lifted her brow in question.

"Boots was about all she could handle."

Annie's chest grew tight as tears stung her eyes. "I called every Friday. I knew her age slowed her down." In hindsight, Annie blamed herself for not noticing anything in Gram's words to indicate she needed her. Wrapped up in her own grief, she completely missed it. "If she needed help, I wish she'd have told me."

She swallowed hard, pushing down the guilt. With the free time she had, it would have been easy for her to head north. "I spoke to her a week before she died. Just one word from her, and I would have been here immediately."

"I can see that." Alice's tone softened. "If it makes you feel better, I pitched in whenever she let me. She asked me to plant these impatiens. But of course she was a bit stubborn."

"A bit? Try a whole lotta stubborn."

They both chuckled, which went a long way in patching up Annie's heart.

"So how long are you staying?"

"Honestly? I don't know." Without a concrete goal, she decided to take it one day at a time. She'd had a place here once. What about now? "I made arrangements when the lawyer called, but that's about as far as my plans go. I guess

I'll stay as long as y'all will put up with me."

Alice chuckled, that infectious sound Annie remembered so well.

"What?" asked Annie.

"You've been gone a long time. Love the accent," said Alice.

"Yeah, I've picked up a word or two."

"You're not in Kansas or, in your case, Texas, anymore."

"Believe me, I know that's true. The clerk at Hansen's asked me to repeat myself at least three times when I asked how he was doin'."

"People will warm up soon enough." Alice shifted from one sandaled foot to the other. "Your grandmother didn't blame you for not coming up here. She knew you had your family to worry about."

"Sounds like you knew her pretty well."

She shrugged. "A few years ago I moved next door—in what we used to call the carriage house, though Betsy had sold that corner lot. I was going through a rough patch, a divorce actually, and I spent some time with Betsy."

"So you were one of her strays?"

"Afraid so." A wistful smile passed over Alice's face. "I appreciated her advice and wisdom."

"Even though I didn't get back here, trust me, I called her often for just the same. She really knew how to take a problem and turn it around to the positive."

"That's why we all loved her."

Annie took hold of Alice's hand. "Thanks for being there for Gram."

Alice patted hers. "I'm sure I got more out of the time

I spent with her. She was a special lady."

They stood in compatible silence for long moments before Boots returned, wrapping herself around Annie's ankles.

"Boots has been with me since Betsy passed. I'm sure she'll be glad to be home again."

"And I can use the company. It's going to take some getting used to, roaming around the big house without Gram here."

"I saw a bag of cat food in the pantry. Just in case Boots decides to split her time between Grey Gables and my place, I'll keep the bag I bought."

"She's that finicky?"

"You have no idea."

Annie placed a hand over her stomach. "Speaking of food, I need to get some. Hansen's didn't have much stock. Is Magruder's Groceries still open?"

"Yep. Right along with Malone's Hardware. Mike runs it now. And The Cup & Saucer."

"Still the place to get gossip?"

"Small-town living never changes."

Annie grinned. "I have to stop by Mr. Procter's office in the morning. I'll get reacquainted with the town tomorrow."

"I'm so glad you're here," Alice said, finally warming up to her long-lost friend. "It'll be nice to get to know each other again."

Annie thought she noticed a glint of hope in the other woman's eyes. She knew the feeling. "I agree."

Her smile brightened. "Well, you must be exhausted after your long trip. I need to get back home. But if you need me, I'm just next door." She pointed down the driveway to the right. Annie could just make out a roofline through the heavily leaved trees separating their properties.

"Thanks, Alice. I'll certainly take you up on that."

Annie watched Alice walk away. Contentment washed over her, filling the empty void she'd lived with for so long now.

Turning on her heel, she hurried back into the house. "Boots," she called, "let's get acquainted."

Boots raced by her, tripping her slightly as she crossed the threshold. "I take it we're friends now?"

While Boots shot down the hallway to the kitchen, Annie headed upstairs, anxious to see her old bedroom. There were four bedrooms upstairs, hers being one of the smaller ones. It hadn't changed much, a single bed with a brass headboard and a dresser she'd painted during her last summer there. She'd begged and Gram gave in, never expecting Annie to choose hot pink as her color. Still, it matched the pink flowered wallpaper.

She smiled as she headed to the master bedroom. In this room Gram had left her mark. A quilt rack, piled up with mostly discarded clothes instead of quilts, angled against the far wall. A pearl necklace and gold clip earrings, along with perfume bottles, were scattered on the dresser top. The closet door was slightly ajar, revealing a pair of tattered slippers. It was as if everything remained the same, waiting for Gram to stroll back in and resume her life.

Like always, Annie was drawn to the window that overlooked the front yard. She opened the window, taking in the outstanding view of the ocean. She could hear the waves breaking on the rocky shoreline. Seagulls dipped into the water, looking for a meal.

Fighting the unshed tears, Annie crossed the room and sat on the bed, enjoying the silence while she gently brushed her fingers over the time-worn patchwork quilt. She gratefully noticed that someone had put fresh linens on the bed. Probably Alice. Her mind turned to memories. She'd spent lots of time here, sitting on Gram's bed as they chatted about life, hopes, and dreams. Back then, she knew exactly what she wanted, knew how she wanted to make her mark on the world. What had happened to that girl? Annie didn't know, but maybe in this place, she could find herself again.

A loud thump broke her musing. In the quiet room, the noise reverberated, making her heart jump. "What in the world?"

The sound came again, followed by a faint meow.

"Boots?" Annie stepped into the hallway and listened. Nothing but stillness and the occasional creak. She moved cautiously down the hallway, noticing a slightly open door.

"Boots?" she called again.

An answering thud coming from the attic greeted her.

"So that's where you ran off to."

She eased open the door and made her way up the steep stairway to the attic, sneezing when she reached the top. Just as she remembered, clutter filled every available space. Clutter and dust. Gram had kept everything she ever owned, plus other people's belongings, stored here. How many rainy days had Annie spent up here during her summer visits, hunting through treasure after treasure? Or playing dress-up with Alice after finding a box of old skirts and scarves? Oh, the tea parties she'd held using mismatched china found in an old wooden box.

Annie carefully weaved through the tiny path until she found the pull string hanging from the lone ceiling light. She tugged. Illuminated now were bulky items wrapped in sheets and tucked under the eaves, odds and ends Gram always said she'd keep in the family. It would take weeks to go through all this stuff. Okay, make that months.

Annie groaned. "Oh, Gram. What were you thinking?"

Overwhelmed by the sea of boxes, Annie stood stunned among years of collections her grandmother had taken to heart and stored here for future generations. Antiques. Crystal and china. Crocheted afghans. Her eyes misted, and she wished Gram were here so they could uncover each and every secret together.

It was all too much to deal with so soon. She turned to leave. And that's when she noticed a large, sheet-covered object in the corner. It was set between a trunk and an old washstand, almost as if protected from the rest of the jumble. Compared to everything else up here, the sheet looked relatively new, with very little dust. Curious, she tugged the sheet free. What it revealed made Annie gasp.

In a roller frame, the largest, most detailed cross-stitch she'd ever seen featured a woman sitting on a porch. As she bent to look closer, she realized it was her grandmother's handiwork. Yet somehow this piece had a different feel to it, like nothing Annie had seen in Gram's work before. The technique, colors, and texture took on a life of their own, almost as if it were a watercolor painting. Incredible.

With a loud meow, Boots came leaping from some hidden spot. Annie nearly toppled the frame as she jumped, catching hold of it just before it hit the ground. Making sure the piece stood safely upright, she covered it again and made her way back to the stairs, hurrying after the cat.

"Okay, okay, I get the message," she yelled after the cat, her heart racing. "I'll feed you. But first, you and I are going to have a long discussion about scaring me in the future."

She followed Boots into the kitchen, ready to hunt for the cat food. Instead, she found a homemade flyer for the "Got Junk?" man. She picked it up from the counter with shaky fingers.

Suddenly the reason for this trip weighed heavily on her shoulders. She'd barely been able to sort through Wayne's things, sort through her own life to see how she now fit in the world. How could she possibly conquer all this?

"One stitch at a time." She repeated the mantra Gram had uttered whenever she would tackle a mountain-sized task, whether it was a new cross-stitch design or a life-altering crisis. And that's how Annie would deal with this. *One stitch at a time.*

～ 2 ～

By the time Annie's meeting at the attorney's office ended, exhaustion sapped her. Going over the paperwork, worrying about making the right decisions, plus the overlying sadness about not being there for Gram at the end, really drained Annie's energy.

Of course, not having slept well last night might have been part of the problem. The creaks and groans of the dear old house hadn't helped relax her. She'd grown used to being alone, but for some reason being alone *here* felt different. She'd tossed and turned in her old bed, finally giving up to head downstairs for a glass of water then roam around. Eventually she'd ended up in Gram's bed where she finally settled down, only to rise with the sun and prepare for the meeting with the attorney this morning.

Now she stood on the steps outside the law office, in need of a coffee break.

Mind made up, she strolled the two blocks to Main Street, made a turn, and headed directly toward The Cup & Saucer. A row of lampposts, straight out of a Dickens novel, created welcoming beacons along the aged sidewalk. The thoroughfare appeared exactly as she remembered; a typical New England downtown, quaint and long lasting. Parking spaces lined the street, providing customers with easy access to the diner, Steiner's Shoe Repair, Finer Things, an

upscale housewares store, and Dress to Impress, the premier dress shop in town—just to name a few. Town hall and
the Town Square were situated about midpoint. Old Glory
flew proudly over the Town Square. Annie recalled many
Fourth of July celebrations there, especially the fireworks.

She made her way down the street, glancing through
windows. Alice was right, many of the businesses were just
as she remembered, though maybe the storefronts had been
updated with time. Annie recalled dashing up and down
the sidewalk when she was younger, running errands with
Gram—stopping at Magruder's Groceries, where old man
Magruder would hand out penny candy to the children on
Saturdays, or the Stony Point Library, holding the annual
summer Read-a-Thon. Annie loved to read, but she especially loved the big blow-out party at the end of the summer,
just before she headed home to Texas. Balloons, hot dogs,
and a free book—what pleasant memories. And, of course,
The Cup & Saucer had been a frequent stop. Where else
could a girl get a stack of blueberry pancakes as tall as she
was? As Annie pushed open the door, she was greeted with
the familiar chime of a cow bell over the door, along with
the scent of fresh-brewed coffee and sizzling bacon.

"Mornin'," a waitress called out. Annie waved before
wending her way to the only vacant table in the corner,
taking the laminated menu from its place between the
salt and pepper shakers in the shape of cows and pigs. A
plump, younger woman in a pink uniform with a white
frilly apron scurried over, a harried air about her, with
coffeepot in hand. Tucking her short dark hair behind one
ear, she poured the rich brew into the mug already placed

on the table. "Hi. I'm Peggy. What can I get you?"

"Just wheat toast, light butter."

The woman eyed her a bit warily, then nodded and headed to the kitchen.

With a sigh, Annie poured a bit of cream into the coffee and took a sip. "Ahh," she murmured, hoping the caffeine worked its magic quickly. After another swallow, she set the mug down and surveyed the room. The noise level had lessened, and if she didn't miss her guess, all eyes seemed to be regarding her, if a bit covertly. She hid a smile, realizing that she was indeed an outsider and would therefore be treated to undue scrutiny. She'd expected this, especially when Mr. Procter had warned her of this very reaction not more than thirty minutes ago. And since The Cup & Saucer was more of a local hangout than a tourist haunt, she didn't expect any less. Still, the humor of the situation didn't escape her.

Peggy returned shortly. "Here's your toast," she announced, setting the plate on the table. Annie noticed that she hesitated. Peggy was working hard to keep her curiosity in check, but it won out after a few seconds. "Visiting someone in town?"

"Actually, I'm staying at Grey Gables. Betsy Holden was my grandmother."

Peggy's gaze warmed a bit. "We were all sorry about Betsy. She was a popular lady around here."

"I know. I spent summers here when I was younger."

"Really?"

"Sure. I used to pal around with Alice, um, MacFarlane. I believe that's still her last name?"

"For the time bein'." Peggy glanced around the room, then back to Annie. "So where are you from?"

"Texas."

"You're a long way from home."

Might as well make nice so the good people around here wouldn't treat her like a stranger, Annie thought. "In miles, yes, but Stony Point has always held a special place in my heart."

"Here for long?"

"I'm not sure, but I'll let you know when I figure that out."

A slight smile turned the woman's lips. She nodded at Annie's mug. "Need a refill?"

Annie nodded and the waitress hurried off for the pot. When Peggy reached the coffee station, she whispered to another woman dressed in a matching uniform, who then spoke to a couple seated at a table near the window. Just as Annie had expected, the rumor mill had begun. And Annie knew her indecision about staying would just add fuel to the fire.

How do I figure all this out? she wondered for the hundredth time. Being stuck in this limbo made her out of sorts and lost. She didn't like this feeling, not one little bit. She'd always been a take-charge type. When she and Wayne had run the business together, she always had a clear-cut goal and a plan to get there. But now, it was as if all the events that had happened during the past couple of years had left her at a standstill. Instead of getting easier, her indecision was getting worse.

If she were home, she'd probably call LeeAnn and get together so she could talk things out. That's what they'd always done before. But Annie was in Maine and LeeAnn was in Texas. She didn't want to burden her daughter with her concerns, especially when Annie hadn't quite figured out what those concerns were.

A deep throbbing started in her temple. Great, now she was giving herself a headache. Not the best way to start the day.

After taking a bite of the toast, Annie decided to bite the bullet and read the legal documents Mr. Procter had given her. Gram had laid out everything plainly; Annie inherited the house and land. There were no stipulations that Annie must reside in Stony Point to keep the house, nor that she should never sell the house under any circumstances. Gram preferred to keep Grey Gables in the family but left the decision making in Annie's capable hands. There were other odds and ends—nothing Annie couldn't handle.

Still, the nagging feeling that she was missing something, something unsaid on Gram's part, bothered Annie. Probably one of the reasons she'd had trouble sleeping last night. What was she going to do? Again the question plagued her as it had when she'd first arrived and walked through the house. The thought of selling Grey Gables didn't set well, but what would she do with two houses? Split her time between Maine and Texas? And what about LeeAnn and the twins? Did Annie want to be so far away from them? On the other hand, the thought of them visiting her in Maine warmed her heart. Especially during the summer months. She could make new memories with her family in the house she loved. The thought definitely appealed to her.

But Grey Gables had seen better years. Annie was no handyman, as her husband had teased her through the years. She wasn't allowed to use a hammer or screwdriver on any important home-improvement job. Wayne had always handled the tools, especially after he caught her hammering a nail in the wall with his "good" wrench. It wasn't that Annie was clueless; she just didn't have the aptitude for construction. Needlecrafts? Yes. Honey-do lists? Well, she made them; she didn't execute them.

Annie put away the paperwork, finished her coffee, and paid her tab. With all eyes still flitting her way amid the hushed chatter about the new girl in town—who really wasn't so new—she paused at the door and waved back at the room. She chuckled at how busy everyone suddenly became. The townsfolk knew she was back, that's for sure.

With the intention of stopping at Magruder's, she headed south down Main Street. She hadn't made it very far when a new shop—well, new to her anyway—caught her interest. Stenciled on the wide storefront window was the name, *A Stitch in Time*. Intrigued, Annie peered inside. From her vantage point she could make out floor-to-ceiling shelving, a counter near the door with an old-time cash register, and a cozy circle of overstuffed armchairs. Despite her need for groceries, Annie pulled open the frosted glass door. Had she entered paradise?

She inhaled the pleasant aroma of polished wood, fabric dye, and glue, scents that Annie had grown up with and associated with her grandmother. Stepping farther into the cool interior, her footsteps echoed on the hardwood floor. She stopped beside the counter, her gaze roving from the shelves of color-coordinated yarn, to a free-standing display featuring embroidery floss and aida cloth. An entire wall housed pattern books, and the latest issue of *Crochet World* graced the front counter. Another wall held a selection of needles, hooks, scissors, and other essentials for craftwork. Deeper into the store were bolts of fabric and a wide array of quilting supplies.

"May I help you?" a voice asked from the back of the store.

Annie turned in that direction. A stocky woman with salt-and-pepper hair approached, stopping by the front counter to replace the receiver of a wireless phone. "I'm Mary Beth Brock. Welcome to A Stitch in Time."

"Your store is wonderful. I don't know where to start browsing."

"Spoken like a true needlecraft enthusiast."

"All my life. I'm Annie Dawson."

The woman smiled and tilted her head toward the counter. "So I just heard."

Annie realized the woman must have just gotten off the phone with someone at the diner. "News travels fast."

"In Stony Point, it does."

"Then you must have also heard that my grandmother was Betsy Holden."

"Dear Betsy. Oh, I just loved her." She reached over to pat Annie's arm. "I'm so sorry about her passing."

"Thanks. Did my grandmother spend time here?"

"Not lately, but in years past we spent many hours together. She taught beginner classes and eventually formed the New England Stitch Club right here. Did you know there are about fifty chapters in the region now?"

"That many? No, she never mentioned it. I knew about the club, though. She loved visiting other needlecrafters, but I didn't realize how far the stitching network extended."

"That was Betsy. Big ideas and yet modest to a fault. She loved sharing her gift."

"And it was a wonderful gift. Her cross-stitch designs always resembled watercolor paintings to me. I don't know how she did it. I shouldn't have been surprised, but the depth of her scenes always amazed me."

"And the stitches she used." Mary Beth shook her head. "Very innovative. Always just a bit different from the usual cross-stitch to give it a little something ... special. And secret. She wouldn't share her special technique with anyone. Which always made her work in demand. I wouldn't be surprised if a book featuring a compilation of her designs comes out now that she's passed." Mary Beth sighed. "A Betsy Original is always quite popular and will be even more so now that there won't be any new works."

Annie's thoughts flashed to the cross-stitch she'd come across in the attic. Should she tell Mary Beth? It could very well have been her final piece. Annie made a mental note to really study it thoroughly once she got home before saying anything.

"Betsy was a remarkable woman, and I'm glad you've come here," said Mary Beth. "She spoke quite highly of you over the years, you know."

Touched, Annie placed her hand over her heart. "She did?"

"Yes. She was proud of the life you'd created, and bragged often about her granddaughter and great-grandchildren. She always stopped in whenever you sent new pictures."

"Which was as often as I could take them."

"She missed you," Mary Beth said quietly.

"And I missed her. Even talking to her once or twice a week wasn't enough."

"Hey, she was happy with those calls. She knew your life was in Texas. I guess she just got lonely once in a while."

Annie could certainly relate to that. After Wayne died, she thought she'd go crazy with the loneliness. "But you kept her busy?"

"More like the other way around!" Mary Beth's eyes grew moist. She cleared her throat. "So what's your favorite needlecraft?"

"I love to crochet." She nodded at the wall of yarn. A rainbow of colors, captured in multiple skeins and different textures, would lure any needlecraft lover. "You have serious inventory here."

"As you might say in Texas, 'We aim to please.'"

Annie chuckled. "You'd be right about that." She pointed to the bolts of fabric in pastels, rich hues, and bold colors and patterns. "I began quilting a few years ago but never devoted much time to it."

"If you plan on staying in town, now might be the time to start a quilting project. The summer classes I offer will begin soon."

"I'm afraid I won't be able to swing it. I was planning on visiting only a few weeks, but I'm surprised at the condition of the house. So I may have to lengthen my stay."

"And we're thrilled to have you."

"Thanks." Annie wandered toward a circle of chairs to the right of the front door. Bright sunshine spilled in from the big picture window, casting the furniture in a warm, welcoming pool of light. "Do many people come here to relax?"

"Sometimes. Folks drop in to browse and visit, but the circle is usually reserved for the needlecraft club that meets here every Tuesday at eleven. We call ourselves the Hook and Needle Club. You should come."

The thought of meeting and making new friends appealed to Annie. A way to connect with her grandmother by spending time with other women who knew her. Maybe find a place to fit in. Figure out the next step in her life.

A tingling of anticipation warmed her. "I could use the company."

"Then it's set. I won't accept no for an answer."

Annie didn't doubt it. Mary Beth seemed more than capable of making sure Annie joined the group.

"And while I'm here, I need some yarn." Annie glanced over at the wall of color. "I don't even know where to begin."

"You're talking to the right person." Mary Beth, the consummate shop owner, strode briskly to the yarn section. "Just tell me what you're working on, and we'll go from there."

"A baby blanket," she told Mary Beth, following her to the yarns. As Annie passed a dressmaker's mannequin adorned with a beautiful crocheted jacket, she stopped. Deep magenta, rose, and pink in a striped design, edged in chocolate brown; it rivaled anything she'd seen in trendy boutiques back home.

"This is gorgeous."

"Thanks," Mary Beth beamed. "I can't take the credit, though. Kate Stevens, my employee, designed and crocheted this."

"She's quite talented."

"Yes, she is. And modest about her talent as well. I finally talked her into displaying her work for customers. She's even gotten a few custom orders. She's also part of Hook and Needle. You'll meet her Tuesday."

Annie fingered the soft yarn and grinned. "How could I resist?"

*   *   *   *

An hour later, loaded down with grocery bags, Annie pushed open the front door with her foot and made her way down the hallway. Boots nearly tripped her once as she entered the kitchen, her loud meows demanding lunch.

"Hold your horses there, kitty. I'll get to you."

She filled the cat bowl with crunches, then put the groceries away, thinking the entire time about the cross-stitch upstairs in the attic. Once finished with the kitchen task, she headed up to the attic instead of making lunch. After talking to Mary Beth, curiosity burned in her, and she knew she couldn't eat a thing until she checked it out to see if this was indeed Gram's work.

Carefully making her way to the light, she pulled the string and headed straight to the covered frame. Slowly, she pulled off the sheet. The dim lighting did little to illuminate the cross-stitch, so she picked up the framed piece to carry down to the living room. The natural light there would be much better to examine the piece.

A plain envelope fluttered to the ground as she lifted the frame from the stand. Had it been tucked into the wood, disturbed when Annie lifted the frame? With her arms full, she ignored her growing curiosity. The envelope would have to wait. Once downstairs, she set the frame on the couch and hurried back for the frame stand, picking up the envelope along the way.

Back in the living room, she dropped the envelope on an end table and placed the stand at an angle near the window—not too close to ruin the material—with the best diffused lighting. She set the frame with the cross-stitch against it. Stepping back, she viewed the project. "Gram, how beautiful."

In this lighting, Annie could make out more clearly a young woman seated in profile on a porch swing, next to a window, staring off into the distance. How did Gram capture the soulful gaze of the woman in the stitchery? The image had an ethereal quality that drew her in. Annie couldn't help but wonder, what was the woman—well, young lady really—thinking at that moment?

The woman gazed off into the distance. The clothes were of a different era, a pale pink blouse with a high collar and a navy skirt. Her hair, swept up at the back of her head and fastened by a filigree barrette was too formal for today's woman. She couldn't have been more than a teen.

As she stepped back to get a better view of the cross-stitch, Annie assumed the location was Grey Gables. Just to make sure her guess was correct, she went out to the porch and hunted for the spot that featured the swing. When she found the general direction the young woman in the stitching was staring at, the hill at the end of the property leading down toward the rocky shoreline, she was sure she'd found the exact window beside the woman stitched on the cloth.

Okay, she'd found the window, but no porch swing. This had to be the spot. The details on the cloth were as clear as a snapshot. Looking up, Annie spied holes in the ceiling that might have anchored a porch swing at one time. She compared the view again. No doubt about it, the woman was indeed at Grey Gables. Satisfied with her search, she hurried inside.

Annie puzzled over the young woman in the cross-stitch once more, trying to discern the source of the feeling that something was ... off. And then it hit her. Gram never stitched people. Only places.

Which moved this piece into a whole new realm.

She continued studying the woman and eventually noticed small individual scenes that she initially overlooked while concentrating on the young lady. The stitches were so small and precise that when she moved to the other side of the room, the finished scenes resembled a photograph. A beach, a barn, a storefront, and a house. None of the images looked familiar to her. She'd covered a lot of ground when she was younger and thought she knew Stony Point well. Still, nothing came to mind in her patchwork childhood memories. Could they be local places or just part of a pattern? This was Gram's work, of that Annie had no doubt, especially with her initials neatly stitched into the bottom right-hand corner. And her grandmother had always patterned her scenes after real places. Just because she didn't recognize the ones stitched here didn't mean they didn't exist.

What did all this mean? And who was the woman? It certainly wasn't Gram. Or anyone Annie recognized as family. Yet the girl's gaze haunted her. The emotion stitched there was so real. Annie longed to know what it meant.

Wasn't it just like Gram to keep Annie busy even though she wasn't here? Just like all the summers Gram would come up with a plan to keep Annie occupied, either with a new crochet project, redoing the vegetable garden, or digging a new flower bed. There hadn't been one summer when Annie had been bored.

"Looks like you came up with another project for me, Gram."

And, as usual, Gram's timing was right on the mark. Annie needed a distraction from her indecision about the direction of her life. What better way to forget her problems than by figuring out what Gram had meant by this cross-stitch piece?

Totally hooked, Annie studied the woman again.

"Who *are* you?"

— 3 —

With a whirlwind of questions running through her head and hunger growling in her stomach, Annie decided to take a break. Heading to the kitchen with the intention of making lunch, she passed an antique wall clock, only to realize it was nearing three o' clock. she'd been so caught up in the mystery cross-stitch that the afternoon had flown by. She decided to slice Colby Jack cheese to snack on with crackers while Boots weaved between her feet, clearly angling for more food. "Don't get any ideas, cat."

Making her way back to the living room with her snack and a glass of lemonade, she took a few bites before noticing the forgotten envelope on the end table. Setting the plate down, she reached for it just as the doorbell rang.

"Hold your horses," she called out as she jogged into the foyer, opening the door on the third ring.

"Hey, neighbor."

"Alice. What a nice surprise. What brings you over here?"

"Heard you were in town today."

"It's uncanny how fast news travels around here." She chuckled as she ushered her friend inside. "I feel like a celebrity with the buzz going on about my presence."

"It's just that people are surprised you're here. They're worried about what you're going to do with Grey Gables." A genuine grin relaxed Alice's taut features. "Besides, they don't really take well to outsiders. Tourists passing through— in inns and bed and breakfasts—are one thing. Newcomers with out-of-state plates in their neighbors' driveways, that's something else. It's not a mean thing, just the small-town attitude. People are cautious, that's all. But on the plus side, Mary Beth enjoyed your visit."

Annie smiled inwardly. She could imagine the shop owner calling her friends the minute Annie left the yarn shop, giving the details of their conversation. "Come sit down," Annie invited, leading the way into the living room.

The moment Alice walked into the room she caught a glimpse of the framed cross-stitch. "Oh, is that a Betsy Original?"

"Yes. I found it up in the attic."

Alice crossed the room, stopping before the frame. "I've never seen this."

"Neither have I. I sort of stumbled over it." Annie explained how she'd chased Boots into the attic and found the cross-stitch.

"Your grandmother always did such beautiful work."

Annie joined her friend, standing to one side. "Every time I see one of her designs, it takes me back to a different place and time. When I'm at home, and something is troubling me, I sit and stare at a meadow scene Gram stitched. It was a favorite spot for my husband and me. I'd sent her a picture, and she created the scene on cloth. After my husband died, I have to admit, I took refuge in staring at that meadow. I can't tell you how much comfort I got from her work. It was like I was transported to that spot, so caught up in the beauty of her work that I forgot about my troubles."

"It must be very peaceful."

"Incredibly so. And I'm proud that she shared her gift with others."

Alice tucked her fingers into the front pockets on her cotton crop pants. "A few months after I moved in next door, Betsy brought over a sampler she'd done for me. I was at a really low point, and the words she stitched were so encouraging: 'To everything there is a season. A time for every purpose under heaven. Keep your head held high and your heart ready for love.' She had a knack for knowing just what to do or say to uplift a person. She'll be missed."

Yes, Gram had that effect on people. Lost in thought, Annie could only imagine the many lives she'd touched with her kindness and grace.

"Huh." Alice cocked her head to one side as she contemplated the cross-stitch.

"What is it?"

"Something is odd. I can't put my finger on it."

Annie grinned knowingly. "Keep trying."

"Wait. Betsy never stitched people."

"Bingo."

Alice moved closer. "And the little scenes. What do they mean?"

"I've been trying to figure it out myself," Annie said, taking a seat on the sofa. "So far, no luck."

Alice joined her, kicking off her sandals and tucking one leg under her to get comfortable. "Who's the girl?"

"I don't know. She doesn't look familiar." Annie glanced at Alice. "How about you? Recognize her?"

"Hmm. No." She continued to study the picture. "And

with the way her head is turned, you really can't get the total appearance of her face. This doesn't leave much to go by."

"I've been debating if it's someone in the family or if Gram just made up the design in her imagination. Knowing how Gram only stitched the things she loved, it's my guess she knew this young lady."

"Is there any way to find out?"

Annie shook her head. "All Gram's siblings died years ago. She was the youngest of the family. As they all got older and married or moved on, the family pretty much scattered."

"What a shame you can't find out who she is."

"Who says I can't?"

Alice's brow rose. "What does that mean, exactly?"

"I can ask questions. See if anyone knew about this project."

"Have you learned nothing about our fair town?" Alice wagged a finger at her. "You're an outsider, remember?"

"How much of an outsider can I be? Betsy was my grandmother, and she lived here forever."

"She did. You didn't. Big difference."

"I'm related."

"That won't loosen tongues."

Annie quieted. As a thought occurred to her, a slow smile spread over her lips. "You aren't an outsider, though, now are you? You could help me."

Alice held up one hand. "Hold on a minute. I may have lived here my whole life, but since the divorce, things are … strained."

"I'm sorry. I didn't know."

Alice shrugged. "I'm getting used to it."

Alice might act as though it—whatever *it* was—was no big deal, but Annie begged to differ. She knew a thing or two about deflecting one's true feelings. And if she didn't know any better, she'd say Alice was covering up the depth of hurt over her divorce. But Annie wasn't going to get into that now, at least not until she had a few more facts. And more time spent with her friend.

"I'm going to be here for a while, so the townspeople will have to get accustomed to seeing me around."

"I'm just saying ..."

"Today wasn't so awful. The waitress, Peggy, I think? She spoke to me."

"Peggy's a sweetie. And believe me, the locals pumped her for information as soon as you walked out of the diner."

"It's not like there was anything to tell."

"The fact that you're here in town is a big topic of conversation. Small-town gossip and all."

Annie glanced back at the cross-stitch and pursed her lips. She could be as tenacious as the next person when she set her mind to it. "I'll figure out a way."

"Good luck with that."

Annie chuckled at Alice's skeptical tone. Her friend's reluctance to help—she let it go ... for now. "So, what brought you over?"

"Oh, right. I ran into Mary Beth, and she asked me to bring you to the Hook and Needle Club on Tuesday. Think you can squeeze us into your busy schedule?"

Annie snorted. "Like I'm so busy. Besides, it sounds like fun."

"We thought it might help if you came with someone you

know. I'm planning on being there anyway, so I thought we'd ride together."

"I'd love to."

"You'll like the others too."

"Think they'll be tight-lipped?"

"Count on it."

Annie laughed again. "Then I take it you don't suggest I ask any personal questions."

"Not at your first meeting."

"Point taken."

"Are you going to listen to me?"

"What makes you ask that?"

"I remember a few times when we were kids when you didn't take my advice."

Annie tried, and failed, to remember. "Really? Like when?"

"Like the time you bought those high-heeled sandals at Bascom's Department Store and insisted on wearing them to the Fourth of July bash downtown."

Annie searched her memory. "How old were we? Fifteen?"

"Yep. Right at that confusing age where we wanted to be treated like adults but continued doing childish things."

"True. Then I wore those heels down to the beach when we met a group of kids. Everyone decided to hike from the sand to the rocks."

"Exactly. I told you to wear sneakers." Alice chuckled. "You do recall what happened?"

"I turned my ankle and had to take the sandals off. Then I ended up cutting myself on a sharp stone."

Alice grinned. "You were laid up for a week."

"Not one of my smarter moves."

"We've all had those moments."

"Amen, sister."

They both laughed.

"Is Bascom's still open? I didn't notice this morning when I was in town."

"No." Alice sadly shook her head. "The store closed when the mall went up over on Route 1. They couldn't compete with progress."

For the next hour, the two chatted, catching up on old times. Alice had a previous engagement, so she left before five, leaving Annie to fix a quick frozen lasagna dinner for herself and feed an ever-exasperating Boots. When the cat was hungry, there was no ignoring her.

"I'll bet Gram spoiled you like crazy." Annie leaned down and pointed to the gray feline. "Don't get any ideas. I'm not a soft touch."

Boots meowed in response, then flounced out of the room. That one was bound to be trouble.

Annie spent the next few hours puttering in the kitchen, finally brewing a pot of black cherry tea. Filling a mug, she wandered out to the front porch and perched on a wicker chair. The light faded in the cobalt sky, and the temperature dropped a few degrees, along with the setting sun. Maine summers were like that, she recalled. Warm and toasty, sometimes even hot during the day, but chilly once evening set in. So different from the relentless heat of a Texas summer.

As much as she thought she'd be homesick, Annie found herself looking forward to spending time in town. She hoped Alice was wrong about the townspeople. She remembered everyone as being so friendly. But she'd been a kid then. Betsy's tagalong. Now that she wanted to ask questions, people might forget just who she was. Still, it wasn't going to hold her back. Wayne had always told her she could accomplish whatever she put her mind to.

Annie took a sip of her tea, only to find it had grown cool. As she rose to go back inside for a fresh cup, she noticed headlights on the road. The car slowed at the end of her driveway. Annie stepped from the porch, down the steps, thinking perhaps someone was looking for directions. Suddenly the car accelerated down the street.

Annie stopped, not sure what to make of it. Being so new to the area, she didn't know if she should be concerned or not. Did tourists usually sightsee at Grey Gables? This late in the evening? Or did the fact that an outsider now resided in the Victorian house give someone from town a reason to check it out? She made a mental note to ask Alice.

A little unsettled, Annie hurried inside, securely locking the door behind her before she went to refill her cup. While in the kitchen, she closed and locked the back door. As a woman living all alone, she wasn't one to take chances with her safety. Although this was the kind of town where you could leave your doors open, the passing vehicle had unnerved her.

Returning to the living room, she switched on the lamp beside the couch. Her gaze fell to the envelope she'd never gotten a chance to look at.

She dropped onto the couch, covered her legs with the summer-weight afghan draped over the back of the couch, and pulled the piece of stationery from the envelope. A fine-grade paper, it was marred along the bottom half, water stained and crumply. Annie smoothed it, but the permanent wrinkles remained.

The script was scrawled in an elegant, flowing form— very unlike her grandmother's hard-to-read scrawl. Intrigued, she read:

To the Sister of my heart, this is for you.

Though time has separated us, my memories have not. There are so many things I would have liked to share with you. So many things I would have changed, words I would never have spoken. Life passes so quickly. As I grow older, I wish for a way to move back the hands of time. Instead, we move on. We carry the hurts and disappointments with us, until one day the burden becomes too heavy to bear. We should not have to carry them alone.

Which brings me to

The ink smeared, and she couldn't read the remaining words.

"Brings you to what?" Annie asked the empty room. "I can't believe this." She turned the paper over. No writing on the back. "You have got to be kidding me."

Annie studied the writing again. It didn't look like Gram's penmanship, but she couldn't be sure. Near the end of her life, Gram's writing had grown more loopy and even harder to read. This looked familiar, but ... still, there was a nagging doubt. And with all the stuff stored up in the attic—maybe even things Gram stored for other people—did she really know who wrote this? And did it even go with the cross-stitch? She thought it fell from the frame when she picked it up, but had it belonged with some other box or treasure?

Still, a thought nagged at her. The cross-stitch featured the young woman so prominently, especially since her grandmother stitched scenes, not people. Had her grandmother changed her trademark style along the way and never revealed it to anyone? Why would she do that? And what would that mean in regard to this cross-stitch? Had it been meant for someone special?

"Not only did you leave me this house," Annie whispered, "you left me a mystery."

Her gaze strayed back to the frame. "What did you have in store for me, Gram?" Had Gram purposely left the cross-stitch for her to find?

With more questions than answers at this point, she glanced down at the letter. This was a part of Gram's life Annie knew nothing about. And she thought she knew the older woman so well. Obviously not. What other secrets had Betsy Holden kept all these years?

Which begged the next question: Identify the woman or leave well enough alone?

And then it hit her. She needed to do this. Needed to finish what she'd started.

When LeeAnn had married and moved away from home, it had taken Annie a long time to stop missing her. Then, when the twins arrived, Annie had been there to help, but LeeAnn had handled everything so well. She had insisted on taking care of her new family on her own, so Annie hadn't felt needed. Then, when Wayne had died, she'd totally lost her purpose in life. She'd grown inward. Hadn't socialized like she used to. Her world had unraveled, and she hadn't been able to find the right stitch to make it whole again.

Until, that is, she traveled cross-country to Stony Point, Maine, and Grey Gables.

Finding the identity of the girl in the cross-stitch would give her a purpose again. It may not be as important as battling for world peace, but it gave her a task she could carry out. Gave her the resolve that had been lost in her life.

Mind made up, determination stirring in her heart, Annie latched onto this new chapter of her life like a lifeline. "Okay, now think like a mystery-book detective," she muttered. "Clues. I need clues."

She went down the hall to the library and grabbed a legal pad and pen from the small secretary desk. Returning to the sofa, she jotted down thoughts as they came.

Who would her grandmother feature in the cross-stitch?

What did the little scenes mean? Where were they located?

The list went on. By the time she finished putting all her questions on paper, she'd filled up the entire page, making the task seem daunting. "Good job, Annie. Now what?"

She needed to enlist someone's help with this, and the first person to come to mind was Alice. They'd gotten into plenty of mischief when they were younger. Annie decided she'd spring this new adventure on her unsuspecting friend the next time she had a chance to sit down and explain her plan. Just like old times.

~ 4 ~

By Tuesday morning, Annie alternated between excited and nervous about attending her first Hook and Needle Club meeting. She'd just come downstairs when the doorbell rang. She hurried to open the door to a beaming Alice.

"Ready to meet the group?"

Annie chuckled. "Let me get my tote." She grabbed her things from the hall table but stopped to check her reflection in the large, oval mirror mounted by the front door. "Do I look okay?" She'd fussed for an hour before Alice arrived, over her choice of yellow tank top with an embroidered neckline, casual tan linen crop pants, and flat sandals.

Alice grinned. "You're just meeting a bunch of ladies."

"Oh, c'mon, you know we women dress to impress other women. Women are a tougher audience than men."

"True." Alice glanced down at her own outfit: a white eyelet blouse, denim skirt, and mules. "Now you've got me paranoid, and I don't have anyone to impress."

"You look wonderful. They know you. I'm the one trying to fit in."

"You'll fit in too. Mary Beth already likes you, so you're good."

They stepped onto the porch and Annie locked up. "This is really important to me."

"Trust me. They'll love you." Alice placed a comforting

hand on her arm. "And it's relaxing sitting around with the girls. A little conversation. A lot of needlecrafting. What every woman needs in the middle of the week."

Soon they were headed downtown in Alice's flashy Mustang convertible. "Now this is the way to make an entrance," she said as she stepped on the gas. Their hair blew in the wind.

"Showoff."

"At least I have something to show from the divorce."

As Alice pulled into a parking space across from the shop, a shiny, white Lincoln Continental pulled up to the sidewalk. The driver-side door swung wide, and a tall man wearing a baseball cap got out and rounded the front of the car to open the back door. As an elderly woman stepped out, the man took her elbow to help her stand steadily. She patted his arm, said a few words, and walked away. The man closed the door, watched the woman as she disappeared from Annie's view, then got back in the car and eased his way into tourist traffic.

Alice poked Annie. "What are you staring at?"

"Just watching that driver help an old woman out of a Lincoln."

"That's Jason, and his passenger is Stella Brickson."

"And you know this, how?"

"Everyone in town knows that Jason drives Stella around." Alice shrugged before opening the car door to exit. "She never got her license, and Jason was employed by the Brickson family, so he chauffeured her around town when she lived in New York City. When Stella moved to Stony Point, Jason came with her."

"Did she know Gram?" Annie asked as the two walked to the shop.

"Everyone knew your grandmother. Why?"

"Maybe Stella knows something about the cross-stitch."

"I don't know. You can ask her yourself. She's a member of the club. But I have to warn you."

Annie didn't like Alice's warning tone. "About what?"

"Stella's not a real 'people' person. Not real chatty either. She doesn't like to talk about her life, especially since she moved back here about five years ago."

"So she grew up here?"

Alice nodded. "She came back after her husband died."

"Maybe she's still in mourning? That could explain her demeanor."

"After five years? I suppose."

"What else could it be?" Annie pressed.

"You tell me after you meet her."

Annie tried to quell her nervous stomach as they entered the store. Female chatter sounded, along with the ring of the cash register. Mary Beth stood behind the counter, talking with a customer. She waved when Annie and Alice walked in. As they moved into the interior of the shop, Annie noticed two more mannequins with different crocheted outfits. After the introductions, she planned on checking them out.

"Buck up," Alice teased as they moved toward the grouping of chairs. "Heads up, ladies. I brought the newbie."

Four faces looked up from various lap projects to catch Annie in their laser gaze. She was right on time for the meeting, so how early had these women arrived?

"Let me introduce everyone. From right to left, Kate Stevens. She works here."

"I've seen your work and I'm impressed," Annie said.

"I've never crocheted anything more than blankets and simple baby items. I would love to do something challenging, like your beautiful jacket I saw on the mannequin."

Several years younger than Annie, Kate smiled shyly, tucking a strand of shoulder-length dark hair behind her ear. "I'd be happy to show you how."

Alice nodded to the woman seated next to Kate. "Gwendolyn Palmer, your neighbor up the hill."

With sparkling blue eyes and a pleasantly lined face surrounded by severely styled soft blond hair and dressed in exquisite clothing, Gwendolyn said hello.

"You know Peggy from the diner."

The youngest of the group, Peggy finger waved.

"And this is Stella Brickson."

Stella's gray hair, beautifully styled in a short, layered cut, framed a lined, impassive face. A small woman, she sat straight-backed in the chair, very regal, making it impossible to miss that she held court with these women. She merely blinked as she maneuvered her knitting needles and tugged the yarn from a ball stored in the large tote she'd carried into the shop.

"There are a few others who come from time to time, but this is the regular gang," Alice finished. "Gang, Annie Dawson. New to town, but granddaughter of our very own Betsy Holden."

"And we are more than happy to have you," Mary Beth added as she joined the women after her customer left. "I've been looking forward to your joining us."

"Thanks. I feel the same."

"Sit, sit." Mary Beth ushered Annie to an empty chair.

"Tell us what you're working on."

"A baby blanket. For one of the young mothers at my church back home."

"Texas, right?" Gwendolyn asked.

"Yes. Near Dallas."

"I always wanted to go there." Gwendolyn lowered her needles and stared across the shop. "John doesn't like the heat. But I would love to see the Alamo. Or a real live cowboy."

The other women chuckled.

"I've known a cowboy or two in my day," Annie told her. "When they get done up right in a Stetson and spurs. I expect your men wear lots of wool once the weather changes."

"Oh, yes." Peggy rolled her eyes.

Annie turned her attention back to Gwendolyn. "What are you working on?"

"I knit scarves or lap blankets and donate them to Elderly Services. They hand them out to nursing homes, assisted living facilities, and the Senior Center." Gwendolyn crossed the yarn over a needle. "My parents have passed, but I was close to them, so I understand the need for donations to these services. I get real enjoyment by helping elderly folks." Gwendolyn tugged yarn from the ball on her lap. "Especially my mother-in-law. She lives in Bangor. Since my children are all grown and off living in different cities, we visit her pretty often. I bring the scarves and blankets to a group over there. I love visiting her, but it sure isn't a vacation."

"I'd give anything for a real vacation," Peggy grumbled. "But instead I get Tuesday mornings off to work on my quilting. Between working at the diner and keeping up with my six-year-old, Emily, this is about all the time I have to concentrate on this patchwork bedspread. By the time I finish, Emily will be a teenager." She sighed. "I hope we go on a vacation before then."

"The teen years come soon enough. Don't rush it." Kate rummaged through a box of merchandise at her feet. "Vanessa, my daughter in high school," she clarified for Annie, "would pitch a fit if we went anywhere. She's got the entire summer planned out."

"Besides, Harry will be busy scalloping, so you're stuck here too," Peggy added.

Kate's lips grew tight, but she didn't comment.

"And," Gwendolyn added, "the tourist rush is in the summer, so we all stay close to home."

"Will you be here all summer?" Mary Beth asked Annie.

"I'm planning on it. Grey Gables needs some work, and I'd like to spend time getting the place in order."

"You picked a wonderful time of the year to visit," Gwendolyn said. "Fourth of July is right around the corner. Then there's berry picking and going to the beach."

Alice chuckled as she pulled out a large piece of aida cloth and her cross-stitch. "You sound like a sound bite for a tourist commercial."

"We all have to do our part." Gwendolyn eyed the other woman in all seriousness. "Well, we do."

"Gwendolyn's husband, John, is the president of the Stony Point Savings Bank," Mary Beth explained. "A more civic-minded couple you have yet to meet."

"And promoting activities in the town is part of our duty. We take it very seriously."

"Which works for me," Mary Beth chimed in. "The

more tourists that walk through that front door, the better my bottom line."

Annie twined the pastel pink yarn around the hook to add another stitch, enjoying the women's small talk. She'd been so out of things back home. Maybe this was a place she could relax, enjoy herself and, with new friendships, figure out what to do with her life.

When Mary Beth belted out a laugh, Annie viewed the faces of the other women. Every one was smiling, enjoying herself, with the exception of Stella. She hadn't said one word since Annie arrived, and Annie wondered if the woman was always so silent. As Annie's eyes met the older woman's, she felt the wariness radiating from across the circle. Their gaze held momentarily. Stella pointedly looked away. Confused, Annie wondered what she'd done to garner such a guarded stare, then she remembered that she was the lone outsider in the group.

The conversation turned to Betsy and her Originals.

"I had Betsy come to the shop many times to teach a beginner class or talk about her work," said Mary Beth. "Everyone loved her."

"Really," Kate added, her words hitched. "We packed out the store on those days."

Gwendolyn nodded. "She was certainly talented."

"But she's no longer with us," said Stella, her stilted voice silencing everyone. "I've never understood why people insist on dwelling on those who have passed. We certainly have our memories, but it's time to move on. Betsy would want it that way."

All eyes zeroed in on Annie. Why would Stella say that?

Annie didn't want to tread into uncharted water here, but this was her grandmother they were talking about.

"I think it's good to talk about family. There's so much joy in sharing memories, and my grandmother left so many good ones."

"I'll say," Mary Beth chimed in. "After news of her passing got out, I had so many calls from stitching enthusiasts asking about her. The interest in her has skyrocketed. Many collectors are already on the hunt for any of her projects out there. Unfortunately, there aren't many circulating."

Annie immediately thought of the cross-stitch at home and looked over at Alice. As evidenced by her secret smile, it seemed she was thinking the same.

"She never mentioned that she had anything new in the works," Kate said. "I asked her when she was in the store last, and she changed the subject. I wasn't surprised. She was always hush-hush about her projects."

"Maybe she was working on something new and didn't want to spill the beans," Gwendolyn commented as she wound yarn around her knitting needle. "I can't tell you how many times through the years I tried to get Betsy to tell me what she was working on. She'd always give me that sly smile of hers, and I knew I'd have to wait for her newest masterpiece, like the rest of the world. About drove me crazy."

"Or maybe she'd stopped working. I know *I* hardly ever saw her," Peggy said with a twinge of resentment in her voice. She cast a quick glance at Kate, before looking away. "She slowed down a lot as she got older."

"Trust me," Gwendolyn laughed. "It happens."

Although it was true her grandmother was always working on something, Annie remained reticent on the subject. For now.

Stella addressed Alice. "You lived next door. Was she busy?"

"As far as I could tell, but she always made time to talk to me."

"You had to talk to someone. You never come to town anymore," Peggy groused.

"I've been busy." A shadow crossed over Alice's eyes.

"So busy that you ignore your friends?"

"I still come to the Hook and Needle Club."

"Which is a good thing, because we love having you." Mary Beth patted Alice's arm, but Alice didn't look any less unsettled.

The store phone rang, and Kate set aside the prepackaged cross-stitch inventory she was pricing as she rose and crossed the aisle to answer it.

"She's been moody," Peggy observed.

"It's Harry," Gwendolyn whispered.

The women nodded, practically in unison. Must be some kind of insider knowledge. Knowledge Annie hoped to have after she'd been here for a while.

She scanned the room again. For the most part the women had been welcoming.

And then there was Stella. Everything she'd said so far had been ... pleasant, but there was an undercurrent of tension that Annie couldn't put her finger on. Maybe she never would, outsider that she was. Then again, Alice had warned her about Stella.

So much for fitting in.

"I suppose your grandmother was working on some new cross-stitch?" Stella asked grudgingly, if only to be nice.

She flashed an almost honest smile for the woman. "Always. I see you're knitting, but have you ever done cross-stitch?"

Stella turned her nose up. "I only work with good old-fashioned yarn and needles. Your grandmother may have made a name for herself with cross-stitch, but really, most women I know like to create useful things, like this sweater for Jason. Practical, as far as I'm concerned."

"My grandmother's work was art," Annie assured her as pleasantly as possible. She tamped down her exasperation with the older woman, making nice on this first visit with the club.

"Everyone is entitled to their own opinion," Mary Beth said, obviously the peacemaker. "That's what makes this group so interesting. Still, we will miss Betsy."

"It's not healthy to live in the past," Stella replied. "I haven't, and I'm not going to start now."

"That's a shame," Annie remarked deciding to change the subject. Obviously Stella had issues. Maybe her late husband's passing had really been a trial for the older woman. Annie could relate. "I had hoped to find out more about Stony Point, and you ladies seem like the best source."

That statement brought complete silence to the group. Great, she'd put her foot in her mouth. Tough crowd.

"We don't pry into each other's affairs," Stella warned.

"Oh, I wasn't trying to gossip. I'm interested in the history of the town, the people that settled here. I'm not interested in what's going on now. Well, I am, in that I want to be a good neighbor, but not to gossip—"

"Better quit while you're ahead," Alice cut in with a nervous laugh. "What Annie is trying to say is that she wants to learn more about our community. Become a part of it."

"So you're planning on staying?" Stella asked, her back becoming ever more rigid as she sat straight up in her chair.

"I haven't decided yet. Probably through the summer, at least to get things straightened out at Grey Gables."

"That remains to be seen. Grey Gables has seen better days."

"Stella meant that there's a lot of work to be done," Peggy explained, glancing nervously between Annie and Stella.

"I can speak for myself, thank you." Stella eyed Annie. "The house was once grand. Now it just looks … sorry. I don't know what Betsy was thinking, living there when she could barely take care of it."

"It was my grandmother's home. I think she didn't want to live anywhere else."

Stella shrugged. "Selling the place would probably be your best bet. We always get vacationers looking to purchase a summer home."

Annie couldn't imagine selling Gram's beloved home to strangers who would live there only during the summer. "I'll make that decision when the time comes." Annie's voice was casual yet firm. These people might not like outsiders, but they sure didn't have a hard time telling them what to do. Or maybe that was just Stella.

An awkward silence fell over the group. That's when Annie realized the women were waiting for the outcome in this volley of words. Not wanting to make matters worse than they already seemed, Annie clamped her mouth shut.

"On that note," Mary Beth chirped, breaking the unsettling moment, "I think we should talk about our summer project."

"Do you think now is the best time?" Stella asked, her tone as stiff as her bearing.

Everyone glanced at Annie.

Right. The outsider. Let's not talk in front of her.

She glanced at her watch, working hard to cover the unexpected ache the words brought. "Alice, look at the time. Remember I promised LeeAnn I'd call her this morning."

Alice cocked her head. "Call LeeAnn?"

Annie addressed the group in general. "My daughter. She's been curious about Grey Gables." She packed up her crochet, not letting them see her distress. The meeting hadn't gone exactly as she'd hoped, and right now she wanted to go home and lick her wounds.

"Right. LeeAnn." Alice followed Annie's lead and neatly stowed her project away, as Kate returned to the edge of the circle.

Annie stood, trying to make the false smile she mustered seem real. "It was great to meet y'all. I look forward to working with you ladies again."

"Next Tuesday," Mary Beth reminded her, forcing a cheerful note to her words.

"Right," Annie repeated as she caught Stella's frown amid the guarded faces of the other women. "Next Tuesday."

*   *   *   *

With a heavy heart, Mary Beth watched the two women leave the store.

"Well, that was awkward," Peggy said as soon as the door closed.

"It didn't have to be." Mary Beth stared pointedly at the other women before crossing the room to the window. She really liked Annie, wanted her to be part of the club. She thought she'd be a welcome addition. Unfortunately, having lived here so long now, she'd forgotten the small-town wariness of strangers.

"I'm just saying ..." Peggy shrugged.

"She just lost her grandmother," Kate pointed out in a stronger tone than necessary.

"And we should consider that." Mary Beth turned to face the ladies. "We've all been there at some point in our lives."

Stella huffed and dropped her knitting in her lap. "As a newcomer, she can't come into our group and cause dissension." She scanned the group. "Where are your loyalties?"

Mary Beth wasn't surprised by Stella's stance. They'd had plenty of arguments on just this subject. Mary Beth welcomed and encouraged new friends. Stella didn't trust anyone, new or old.

"Our loyalties," Mary Beth said, "are the fact that we all enjoy needlecrafts. Do we need anything else?"

"I'm not taking sides," Kate clarified as she forcefully stuck a price sticker on another package. "But since Betsy just passed away, it's no surprise that Annie would want to remember her. Where else would anyone want to talk about her but here in the very place Betsy endorsed needlecraft products? She loved A Stitch in Time."

"She loved spending time here with *certain* people," Peggy muttered.

Stella bristled "My point, ladies, is that we must be careful. Remember when that woman, what was her name, Sandy something, tried to join the group just to get the dirt on our town?"

"That was Sunny Campbell," Gwendolyn corrected. "She wanted to write an exposé on small-town drama. I read her column whenever John and I are in Bangor. She likes controversy. The more dirty laundry aired, the better."

"And we don't," Stella added calmly. "We protect Stony Point just the way it is."

"That's right," Peggy agreed. "We're a small town and we have our standards. And one of them is not letting an outsider privy to our lives."

Mary Beth couldn't believe what she was hearing. She loved these women, but she didn't love how close-minded they could be sometimes. "Annie isn't a reporter," she reminded the group. "She's a new friend trying to fit in by discussing Betsy. Her grandmother. Her family."

Peggy set down the swatch of gingham fabric she was stitching into her quilt design. "Betsy was one of us. Annie isn't."

"Yet." Kate's cheeks grew red.

Peggy angled toward Kate. "So now you finally weigh in on this?"

She glanced at her boss, Mary Beth, her jaw working.

"Tell us how you really feel," Peggy goaded.

"Ladies." Stella interrupted the squabble, a slight trace of a smile forming. "I think today was just an off day. We got off on the wrong foot. I'm sure Annie didn't mean anything."

Annie didn't mean anything by talking about her grand-mother? Mary Beth thought it should be the other way around. Stella had created the tension, not Annie. Over the years that Mary Beth had known Stella, she'd picked up on Stella's distrust, for lack of a better word, of outsiders. The disdain in her tone or an unflattering frown sent toward an unsuspecting visitor showed Stella's thoughts plainly. Which was odd, since she'd lived more years in New York than she had growing up in Stony Point.

Mary Beth stopped struggling with her thoughts. She wasn't going to change years of inherent attitudes in one afternoon. Nothing would change today. But there was always tomorrow.

"I have a suggestion," Mary Beth said as she paced around the circle of chairs. "Let's start over next week. I'm sure Annie would appreciate it if we gave this another try."

Everyone in the group agreed. Lips pursed, Stella continued knitting without saying a word. Was that a yes or a no?

~ 5 ~

blew it." Annie moaned as she and Alice walked into
Grey Gables.

"Don't worry about them. Actually, for your first visit to
the group, you did pretty well."

"You mean they've done that before? Scared off poten-
tial club members?"

Alice belly laughed. "Oh, yes, they do it all the time.
Look at it as a rite of initiation."

"I don't know if I'm cut out for that."

"Look, I know you want to make friends. Give it time.
It'll take folks in Stony Point a while to get comfortable
with you."

"How long?"

Alice glanced at the clock on the wall as she passed it
going into the living room. "From now? I'd say, oh, about
five years."

Annie sank down into a chair. "Thanks for the pep talk."

"By the end of the summer, they'll forget where you
came from. Look, Mary Beth likes you. Kate and Gwendolyn
warmed up. Peggy can be a real hard sell. And Stella?" Alice
rolled her eyes. "She's tough on everybody."

Annie lightly brushed the upholstery with her fingers,
caught up in her own misery. "I didn't mean to offend anyone. I thought if they knew I was interested in the town,

and not gossip, it would make things easier."

Alice took a seat on the couch, crossing one leg over the other. She snatched up a nearby pillow and held it close. Boots came sauntering into the room, stopping to give them a bored stare before jumping onto the couch and curling up in a ball.

"It will get easier. Besides, there are other ways to get the town history. I know you want to find out who the woman in the cross-stitch is, but you have to accept the way it is. There will be an opportunity to bring it up to the group."

"Speaking of opportunity, I meant it when I said I needed your help with this mystery." Reaching over to the end table, Annie grabbed the pad she'd jotted her notes on and passed it to Alice. "Tell me what you think."

Alice scanned the list. "Detailed."

"Occupational hazard."

"It'll work. Keep remembering what your grandmother used to say. Patience is a virtue."

Annie grinned. "And here I thought I'd mastered that. Apparently not."

"Sometimes it takes time to feel a part of an established group. Even if you're already part of it. I know from first-hand experience."

Alice's comment warmed Annie. She was glad to have Alice on her side, even if she spoke in riddles sometimes. "Okay, that's the second time you've made some sort of cryptic comment about your problems here in town. What's up?"

Alice's lashes lowered as she gazed down at the needle-point pillow in her lap. "Since the divorce I haven't quite settled back into my life."

Annie didn't miss the regret in her friend's tone. Obviously the breakup weighed heavily on her.

"I don't think you ever go back to the way things were after a life-changing event." She, too, had lost her husband, only in a different way. Her voice cracked when she spoke. "I understand the heartache, the longing for life to go back to the way it was." The pain and hours of wishing your loved one would come back, knowing he never would. Her throat closed up and hot tears threatened.

"Maybe it's just me," Alice finally opened up, her voice shaky. "Maybe I'm overly sensitive to the remarks my friends make. All I know is that ever since the divorce, people are ... weird around me and that makes me uncomfortable, which makes people think I'm distant. I guess the rumors flew, and I'm not ready to talk about what happened with anyone." She paused, swiping at her eyes. "Really, I just don't want to get hurt again. It's one of the reasons I don't do much in town anymore, except for the Hook and Needle Club. Sometimes being there is uncomfortable too."

"I wish I could help." Annie pushed out the words that had gotten clogged by emotion. "I'm still dealing with my own loss."

Alice's features softened as she regarded Annie. "I know and I'm sorry. And I thank you, because just listening goes a long way. I haven't really had a friend I could be myself with. And I haven't exactly been a delight to be around, either."

"Then consider me that friend."

Alice laughed. "What a pair we make."

"At least we have each other to be honest with." Annie

wiped her wet lashes. "So I didn't blow it?"

"Nah. They'll come around."

For the most part the ladies had seemed open. The mood of the group seemed to have emanated from one person. "What is it about Stella? Could something have happened when she lived in New York to make her so ... cynical?"

"Like I said, she's like that with everyone. She doesn't like to talk about the past, period. When she came back to town after her husband died, she didn't say a word about him. Made it clear that she wouldn't, either."

"I guess some people have a hard time accepting death." Annie couldn't comprehend that. If you didn't mourn, how did you move on?

"She's rather odd, but the truth is, she's been that way since the day I met her. A bit standoffish one time, friendly another. I can't figure her out, and I don't know if she really has anyone she would call a friend."

"I thought maybe she and Gram might have spent time together. They would have been fairly close in age."

Alice thought about that for a moment, then shook her head. "Not that I recall. Even though this is a small town, I'm not sure if they really knew each other." Alice glanced out the window. "There were times they ran into each other at A Stitch in Time. I never noticed them together. Of course, that doesn't mean they didn't talk.

"Then, over the last months of her life, Betsy stayed close to Grey Gables. She said she had things to take care of at home, and I never pushed for details. I did keep coming by, though. I picked up food for her whenever I went to the grocery store."

"Thanks."

"I'm the one who made out. She cooked dinner for me more than a few times, and I don't have to tell you what a good cook she was."

"I have some of her recipes back home, but I think I'll nose around her kitchen for a few more. We should try out a few of her dishes while I'm here."

Alice sat up straight, her eyes wide. "Hey, I have an idea. We could invite some of the girls over. There's nothing that breaks the ice like a good meal."

Annie didn't want to squelch her friend's idea, but she wasn't sure how well that would go over. If she thought doing needlework around these women was tough, how daunting would it be to cook for them? "I think we should experiment first. I'm pretty good around the kitchen, but I don't want to invite them over and make a mess of a meal, like I made a mess of things today."

"Practice makes perfect."

Annie arched her brow. "What's with all the clichés?"

"I don't know. Whenever I think about Betsy, I remember the things she'd say to me. Seemed appropriate."

"In that case, I don't mind. Gram was a wise woman."

"And she'd be pleased if you followed in her footsteps."

Annie glanced at the cross-stitch again. What large footsteps those would be. Her grandmother had touched the lives of everyone who met her. For Annie, it would be a tall order to carry Betsy's legacy on, especially while still trying to find her place in a skeptical town.

Alice looked at her watch, then jumped up from her seat. "Listen, I have to get home and make a few phone calls. What do you say I come back about six and we go have dinner?"

"Sounds great. Any place in mind?"

Alice grinned like a Cheshire cat. "The Cup & Saucer."

The very name made Annie slump. "I don't know ..."

"Trust me, okay? You've got to show people that you're not intimidated by them."

Annie regarded her friend for a moment. Alice was probably right. She needed to make a strong showing in order to be accepted by this town. It was important for her to try.

With renewed determination, Annie nodded. "See you at six."

*   *   *   *

The dinner crowd was already at maximum capacity by the time Annie and Alice entered The Cup & Saucer. After a few minutes, Annie followed Alice to a recently vacated table located at the front window. A waitress hurriedly removed the empty plates on the table and wiped it down.

"This place sure gets crowded," Annie remarked as they took their seats.

Alice pointedly looked at her watch and scanned the room.

Annie watched her over the menu. "What are you doing?"

"Seeing how long it takes word to get to Peggy that we're here."

Sure enough, Peggy glanced over. She held up one finger, as if to say I'll be there in a minute.

"Not bad," Alice commented. "It only took thirty seconds to acknowledge us."

"Is that a new record?"

"Don't know. I've never timed her before. Never had a reason." She smiled broadly. "I'm really glad you're back in town."

Annie shook her head and grinned. She'd forgotten how much fun Alice could be. Honestly, she hadn't had enough pleasure in her life for quite some time. She always enjoyed herself when she was with her grandchildren, but this was different. Her friendship with Alice reminded her of the carefree days of her youth. Of days filled with sunshine and adventure. And a cohort to get into mischief with. How she missed that.

"Hey, you two," Peggy greeted them as she pulled her pen from her apron pocket.

"Hi, Peggy. What's the special?"

"You'll like it. Turkey and steamed vegetables." She looked tentatively at Annie. "We don't make Tex-Mex meals around here, but I could put in a word to the cook if you like."

"Don't make any special allowances for me. I love any kind of food, so I'll take the special too."

Peggy scurried off to fill the order.

"That was headway," Alice told her. "Usually Peggy goes right for the gossip angle. Instead, she offered you food the cook doesn't know how to make. I think it's her way of warming up to you."

"Then I guess I didn't bomb too badly."

"Told you so. I'm sure Peggy was hoping to ask what

happened after we left the group earlier, but she's too busy right now. Trust me, she'll make time to squeeze some kind of info out of us before we leave."

Annie shook her head. "I've never understood the appeal of gossip. I've always had too much to do to worry about other people's business."

"Stony Point is no different from any other small town. Gossip reigns. Always has, always will. And The Cup & Saucer is gossip central."

Annie considered that. Perhaps The Cup & Saucer should be her new hangout, that is, if she wanted answers to her questions. "Then someone must know who the young woman in the cross-stitch is."

Alice shot her a wary glance. "I thought we discussed this. It's too soon to start asking questions."

"I know. I'm afraid I'm a bit impatient, that's all."

"Why is her identity so important to you?"

"What can I say? I'm a mystery buff."

Alice's unconvinced look said she wasn't buying that.

"I guess I feel the need to do something constructive with my life. More than just fix up Grey Gables, even though that's a worthy undertaking. I just feel like I'm missing something ... vital." Annie had never admitted this out loud, and now she was sorry she did. "Does that sound crazy?"

"Not at all. Everyone needs a focal point in their life."

"Then I guess you do understand."

"I do." Alice tapped her finger against her lower lip. "Maybe we should start with the club, like you wanted. You know, to ease into solving the mystery."

"So that means you're making me go back on Tuesday?"

"Of course." Alice grinned. "Did you think otherwise?"

When their meals arrived, Annie dug in. She hadn't realized how hungry she was until now, having lost her appetite for lunch after the disaster at the yarn shop. The gravy-covered turkey melted in her mouth, and the vegetables were steamed just to her liking. It was as if the cook had prepared the meal to her specifications.

Since she'd been living by herself, frozen dinners or takeout had been the extent of her culinary exploits. The only time she changed her habits was when LeeAnn and her family came for dinner. Which wasn't often, so her talent had grown rusty.

The buzz of chatter from the locals enjoying their dinner set a steady rhythm to the room. Freshly brewed coffee vied with the tantalizing scent of fried foods. Every so often a chair scratched over the linoleum floor as folks finished up and headed back home. By the time Annie had finished the last of her veggies, the room was half empty and Peggy returned to refill their coffee.

Annie held up a hand to stop her before pouring and nodded to her friend's mug. "Think caffeine this late in the evening is a good idea?"

Alice toyed with her mug. "Probably not, especially since I didn't sleep well last night."

"Be right back." Peggy hurried back to the coffee station and returned with decaf to top off their coffee mugs. Then she removed the empty dinner plates.

"Thanks," Alice said as Peggy hustled off to another table. "I had a late phone call, then I stayed awake for a long time."

Annie stirred in sweetener. "Nothing bad, I hope?"

Alice waved off her concern. "Not really. Some nights it happens that way. I start out thinking about one thing, which leads to another, and then I end up contemplating all the world's problems. It's a habit I really need to break."

"Or run for office in Washington."

"Talk about never getting any sleep. No thanks. Stony Point action is about all I can handle at this point in my life."

Annie knew to tread lightly with her friend. "I never asked. Do you have a job?"

"Home parties."

Annie raised an eyebrow in question.

"Home party sales. I started out doing jewelry parties for the Princessa company to make some extra money. I would book dates and tote around all this awesome jewelry. I guess I have a knack for sales because I did very well and got hooked, so I branched out to Divine Décor, home decorating. I'm surprised at how busy it keeps me, but it's flexible. I make my own hours."

"Sounds like fun."

"It is. It gets me out of the house, so I don't dwell on things I have no control over."

Alice didn't say it, but Annie would bet she was referring to her divorce.

"How about you?" Alice asked, returning the topic back to Annie.

"Happily retired bookkeeper. Which is good, since Gram left a whole lot of work behind for me to take care of."

"How are you going to handle that? Good with a hammer?"

Annie grimaced. "Honestly, I'm terrible. Guess I'll have to find help."

Alice took a sip of her coffee. "Oh, you could ask Wally Carson, Peggy's husband."

"Think he'd help?"

"Yep. He's kind of the local handyman." Alice narrowed her eyes and leaned in toward Annie. "But you have to know, Peggy sends him on his jobs with instructions to retrieve as much gossip as possible. So if you don't want anyone to see how your grandmother left things …"

"I'm not worried about that. My late husband and I dealt with employees when we owned the dealership. I can handle nosy people."

"Then ask. Here she comes, but I know that look."

Annie glanced up to see Peggy bearing down on them. "What look?"

"She waited for us to finish eating, but now I guarantee she's going to ask a bunch of questions about what you thought of the club meeting today. Brace yourself."

Truth be told, Annie wasn't up to rehashing the club meeting. It had been a long day, a day when myriad emotions had risen to the surface. "Then now is a good time for a ladies' room run?"

"Good idea. I'll hold her off."

Annie rose and started across the room, only to be stopped a few tables away.

"Excuse me." A man, with neatly cut gray hair and chocolate brown eyes, probably close to her age, rose from his seat. "I saw you sitting with Alice and didn't want to intrude, but I figured you must be Betsy's granddaughter."

"That's right. Annie Dawson. How did—" She stopped midsentence, knowing full well how he knew who she was.

The new kid in town, first and foremost on rumor mill lips. "And you are?"

"Ian Butler. I wanted to offer my condolences. Everyone in town loved Betsy."

"Thank you."

"If you need anything while you're here, let me know." She must have looked at him warily, because he added, "I'm the mayor of Stony Point. I know just about everything there is to know about this town and the people in it."

After today's Hook and Needle Club meeting, she wasn't so sure she wanted to know any more than she did. Still, she did have a cross-stitch mystery to solve.

"Like I said, give my office a call." He smiled genuinely, pulling a business card from his wallet. When she took it from his outstretched fingers, he pointedly glanced at her table. "I won't keep you, I just wanted to say hello."

She nodded and suddenly forgot where she was going. She'd found most people in town had been wary or silent around her. It took her a few seconds to get her bearings straight as she realized that this man was actually friendly.

Ian tilted his head. "Problem?"

"No, of course not." She felt a telltale blush cover her cheeks. What was wrong with her? Finally someone in town willing to give her the time of day, and she gets all flustered. "I'll probably need some help at the house but won't know for sure until I have someone come out and give me an estimate."

"You might want to consider Wally Carson." He nodded over her shoulder. "Peggy's husband. Does fine work."

"So I've heard. Alice already mentioned him, but a

second opinion certainly helps. Thank you."

"Any time."

With that said, Annie turned and continued to the ladies' room. Chuckling to herself, she made a mental note to add another ally to her very short list.

"What took so long?" Alice asked when she returned.

"Got sidetracked."

"Sidetracked?" Alice's gaze passed over the room. "By whom?"

"Ian Butler. He was actually helpful."

"That's our mayor for you, a walking marketing machine for Stony Point."

"Nosy too?" Annie asked, thinking about his remark about knowing everyone in town.

"No, not nosy. He's just really invested here, and he takes his job seriously. You know the sawmill just outside of town? Been in his family for generations. He runs it now."

"As well as being mayor?"

"Yep. And he's good at both."

Annie glanced across the room. Ian was engrossed in a newspaper, *The Point*.

"He also suggested that Wally work at Grey Gables. I should probably ask Peggy if he can stop by."

"He could make the time," Peggy cut in as she sidled up to the table again.

Annie jumped out of her seat, sending the coffee sloshing onto the table. How did she get her timing so right? "Uhh, great. Although I'm not sure exactly what needs to be done."

"Wally's a great handyman. He'll guide you. He can fix about anything." Peggy tore off a ticket from her order pad and handed it and her pen to Annie. "Just write down your number, and he'll give you a call."

The wide, honest smile on Peggy's face had Annie jotting down the number.

As Peggy hurried off, Alice smiled. "I think they could use the extra work." And left it at that.

"And I need the help, so it's a win-win." Annie opened her purse to remove her wallet. "We'd better get going."

Alice stood and grabbed the check. "My treat, remember?"

"Alice ..."

"I insist." Alice turned on her heel and headed to the cash register.

Annie placed her elbow on the table and dropped her chin into her upturned palm, staring out the window. The evening shadows stretched across town, ushering another summer night. The pale blue sky slowly deepened into a rich cobalt. The lighted lampposts sent a hazy glow over the sidewalk. Gram would have loved capturing the small town ambiance for one of her cross-stitch projects. Just like Annie, who was catching that feeling in her heart the longer she stayed in town.

With a smile curving her lips, Annie took a final sip of coffee. She would find a way to fit in here. And she would start with the cross-stitch. Something told her that the young woman featured in the piece would help her do just that.

— 6 —

By the next Tuesday morning, Annie was antsy to get out of the large Victorian house. Her initial appointment with Wally Carson, just shy of a week ago, had been productive but daunting. They'd made a long list of work to be done, and since then they'd worked on the outside. Trim needed to be replaced. The house needed a fresh coat of paint. New plant beds were needed to spruce up the grounds, and the grass needed major rejuvenating. The good news, though, was that the basic structure stood in sound shape. Most of the needed work was cosmetic—a great relief to Annie.

Since painting didn't really require the use of dangerous or complicated tools, she insisted on helping Wally with the trim. He argued at first, until he recognized her determination to spiff up her grandmother's house, and then he gave in.

She had an appointment at the end of the week to meet with her grandmother's banker and go over finances. But for now, she needed a break and made the Hook and Needle Club her destination. She dressed for comfort in a pair of denim capris with an apricot pullover and flat sandals.

She arrived shortly before eleven, hoping to get seated before the others arrived. She wanted to start today's meeting on good footing. She'd decided to be upbeat and willing to fit in. To her surprise, everyone was already there, busy working on their projects. How early did these women arrive? Did they really meet at eleven or were they just pulling her leg?

"Good morning," Mary Beth called out as Annie entered the store. "So glad you came back."

"I wouldn't miss it," Annie told her as she walked to the circle of chairs. "How are y'all this morning?"

"Great, now that Wally has another job." Peggy smiled up at Annie. "Thanks."

"I should be thanking you. I need the help."

"I think I mentioned that Grey Gables was something of a lost cause," Stella remarked in a frosty tone as she stitched away on her sweater.

"Not a lost cause, just in need of a makeover." Annie tried to keep the frustration from her voice but was afraid it hadn't worked. Not five minutes inside the door and Stella was already on her. "Wally and I have great plans," she said brightly.

"Wally once built a bird feeder for me," Gwendolyn announced to the group in general, her eyes never leaving her knitting. "I designed it myself, and he built it. The birds love it. I've had him build three more since then."

That was random, Annie thought.

Peggy chuckled. "I've seen those feeders. They're like vacation homes for birds."

"You should see my seed bill."

Everyone laughed, and the tension ratcheted down a few degrees, thanks to Gwendolyn's bird feeders. Maybe today's meeting would go smoother than last time.

Hoping for just that, Annie took a seat and pulled her

crocheting from her tote bag, covertly eyeing the women in the circle.

Kate didn't say much but kept yawning and rubbing at the dark circles under her eyes. Gwendolyn chatted lightly about her busy weekend. Peggy ran on, aware of the tension flowing from Stella and trying to avert trouble on that front. Alice quietly worked on her cross-stitch, not adding much to the conversation. After Annie's heart-to-heart with Alice, she figured her friend must be having one of those days, a day when she was out of sync and not sure of herself. Annie could relate. She'd had plenty of those days back home in Texas.

"Okay, ladies. I'm all yours until the next customer comes in." Mary Beth dropped into an empty chair. "I'm not complaining, but we've been nonstop since this weekend. The tourists are starting to arrive."

Kate looked up from the ledger book she was writing in. "I know. I'm in the middle of inventory, but I'll take care of anyone who comes in while you're busy with the group."

"Thanks." Mary Beth perched on the edge of the seat, her fingers tapping on her knees. "Okay, here it is. I've been thinking about doing something different for our annual project." She stopped and addressed Annie. "Since you're new to our group, I should probably explain."

Annie nodded encouragingly, her curiosity aroused.

"Every year we work together to make a quilt or an afghan and sell it at the annual Fall Festival. We usually donate the proceeds to a cause close to our hearts."

"Oh, like the Humane Society," Gwendolyn said. "I have two rescue kitties at home, so I always give."

"My charity is the Susan G. Komen for the Cure breast cancer research," Kate said quietly. "My mom had cancer."

"As you can tell," Mary Beth resumed, "we each have our own favorites. But the bottom line is, we always do something together."

"Sounds wonderful," Annie told her, very much liking the idea of giving to the community in one way or another.

"But this year, I want to do something out of the box."

Stella looked up from her knitting. "Why would you want to do that? What's wrong with doing the same as we've always done?"

"I want to shake things up," Mary Beth told her. "Since we have a new member in our group, I thought we should strive for something new."

"That's not what we do," Stella stubbornly replied.

"Just hear me out." Mary Beth's lips turned up into an enigmatic grin. "I think you'll like my idea."

Gwendolyn leaned forward. "Oh my, this should be interesting."

"Here's the plan. We all come up with a personal project. Then we have a contest with all the finished pieces. At the Fall Festival, we let the townspeople vote. Then we auction the top winner off first and the proceeds go to the winner's charity. Next we auction the other projects, and with that total, we donate the money toward something local. Like the Retirees' Fund or Second Harvest or the new children's wing at the hospital. What do you think?"

Silence descended on the group, and then everyone started talking at once, throwing out suggestions and making plans.

"Whoa, whoa," Mary Beth yelled over the noise. "A little order here." The group calmed down. "Remarks? Suggestions? Gwendolyn, you go first."

"I like it," Gwendolyn told her. "Competition makes for interesting results. Betsy and I had our own little competition going, for about as long as I can remember. Well, except for that time ..." She clamped her mouth shut and glanced around the circle. Her eyes widened when she realized she'd said too much. "Let's just say I got a bit carried away trying to uncover Betsy's secret technique, and we didn't speak for a long time after that."

"The whole idea is different," Alice allowed, if a bit hesitant.

Mary Beth turned from Gwendolyn to Alice. "Do I hear a *but*?"

Alice grinned, her face lighting up for the first time since Annie arrived. "But I think you're right, Mary Beth. We should do something out of the ordinary."

Kate nodded. "We'd probably make more money that way and get the entire town involved."

"What do you think, Annie?" Mary Beth turned to her.

Annie held up her hands in defense. "I think I'm the newbie here. You should be the ones to decide. I'll go along with whatever y'all choose."

Stella never missed a stitch. "That is wise. After all, *we've* been doing this for years."

"And from what Betsy once told me, Annie's no slouch when it comes to pitching in for a cause. Besides," Mary Beth leaned over and gestured toward the half-finished baby blanket, "she does impressive work. Why, look at the quality. As fine a job as you'll find by any seasoned needlecrafter."

Annie squirmed in her seat. She did *not* want to be the center of attention or the target of Stella's ire.

"I'm not questioning her ability," Stella defended. "Only her planning involvement, since she's so new to town."

"This time I have to agree with Stella," Annie reluctantly admitted.

Mary Beth regarded her with a disappointed gaze, then jumped up to pace around the circle of chairs. Annie had to admire the woman's enthusiastic energy.

"It's good to have new ideas. That was one thing I could depend on Betsy for. She always came up with something innovative in her work and showcased it in the store."

"That's true." Kate looked up from the ledger. "You just have to look at her cross-stitch work to see that."

"Too bad she didn't show her work to everyone," Peggy grumbled.

Kate's voice took on an edge. "It's not like she left anyone out on purpose."

"Well, she didn't exactly invite everyone to her place to share her ideas."

"She didn't have—"

"Girls," Gwendolyn barked sharply in the universal mother's tone. "Really, it's too bad Betsy didn't leave something behind."

This was Annie's opportunity. Taking a deep breath, she bunched her hands into fists and tried to quell her nervous stomach. "Actually, she did."

All eyes focused on Annie.

Peggy was the first one to break the silence. "So are you going to tell us?"

Annie glanced at Alice, who nodded affirmatively. Taking a deep breath she said, "Betsy left behind a never-before-seen cross-stitch."

Mary Beth gaped at Annie. "What are you talking about?"

"I was up in the attic one day and happened to see a large object covered by a sheet. When I pulled it off, it was a cross-stitch. I'm not sure when my grandmother stitched it, but I have no doubt it's her work."

"And you're only telling us this news now?" Peggy squeaked.

Kate scooted to the end of her seat. "What does it look like?"

"It's a woman sitting on a porch swing at Grey Gables."

Mary Beth wrinkled her brow. "That can't be. Betsy only stitched scenes, not people."

"That's what Annie and I thought," Alice said. "But I've seen it, and the work is beautiful."

Stella set down her knitting. "If your grandmother never stitched people, how can you be sure it's hers?"

"Her initials are in the bottom corner."

"Perhaps someone else did the work and stitched her initials."

"No, I'm sure it's my grandmother's. If you saw the style, you'd know it's a Betsy Original."

"Unless someone copied her style." Stella warmed up to her conspiracy theory. "So much of her work was popular, therefore easy to copy."

"You know, that can happen," Peggy added, her gaze flickering to Stella. "You hear about forgeries all the time."

"I'm sure it is Betsy's work," Annie assured her, keeping her frustration in check. She wanted to remind them that no one could copy her grandmother's style, no one knew her secret. But she remained calm, realizing that no matter the topic, Stella fought every person on every front.

Stella's knitting needles clicked away. "Perhaps you should have an expert check it."

Why was Stella so obstinate about this? Did the woman ever quit? "I think I know my grandmother's style."

"And as I've said, she made pretty pictures, but really, none of it is very functional."

An uncomfortable silence hovered over the women. Annie tried to rein in her temper, but Stella ruined the joy of sharing her discovery with the other women.

"There's a bit of a mystery to this work," Alice told the ladies. "We don't know the identity of the woman in the cross-stitch."

"What do you mean, you don't know her?" Mary Beth asked, clearly intrigued.

"I don't recognize her." Annie let the yarn in her fingers go lax. "It isn't a family member, which you would think it would be, considering she never stitched people."

"Why does she have to be someone you know?" Stella asked. "Maybe your grandmother just put a woman in the scene, simple as that."

"Maybe," Alice said. "But since Betsy never stitched people, to have a woman in this work is different. She must mean *something*."

Mary Beth tapped her finger against her chin. "This certainly is a departure from Betsy's usual style."

"Well, there you are," Stella sniffed. "It can't be an original then."

Annie continued to glare at the older woman. "You haven't seen the cross-stitch. How can you say that?"

Stella dropped her knitting on her lap and glared back at Annie. "I can say whatever I please. This is still a free country."

"In the time I knew Betsy, she had lots of great ideas," Kate said. "Just because this isn't her usual type of work doesn't mean she didn't want to try a new style. Artists do that all the time. You know, stretch themselves."

"Do you know something we don't?" Peggy asked, brows low over her eyes.

"No, I'm just saying we shouldn't jump to conclusions here."

"Ladies, this is a wonderful surprise." Mary Beth quickly tried to douse the flame of contention between them. "Let's not get upset about this. We're only speculating."

"When can we see it?" Gwendolyn asked, anticipation—or was it the spirit of competition?—blazing in her eyes.

After Stella's less-than-enthusiastic response, Annie didn't really want to discuss the cross-stitch any longer. The older woman had sucked the joy out of her announcement.

Alice answered, making the decision for Annie. "It's huge, surrounded by this really heavy frame. There's no way I'd want to lug that thing around."

"Well, there you are," Stella said again as she resumed her knitting. "No need creating an uproar over something we haven't had a chance to see. You wouldn't want to disappoint your customers, Mary Beth, especially if it isn't up to standards."

"I think for now I'll keep it at Grey Gables," Annie told the group.

Disappointment showed on Mary Beth's face. "Oh, I would so love to see it."

"I'll take pictures," Annie told her, not wanting to hurt the shop owner's feelings. Of all the women present, she'd accepted Annie from the beginning, and Annie didn't want to dishearten her. But Annie was still a bit wary, even after her second meeting with these ladies.

Mary Beth smiled widely. "That will have to do. Thank you."

"Just imagine, a new Betsy Original," Kate whispered.

"Wait until this gets around town." Peggy smiled, ready to add new fodder to the rumor mill. "We haven't had this much buzz since—"

"Since the time the Taylor twins painted a mural that was in very poor taste on the side of the Grand Avenue Fish House," Gwendolyn tsked and told them in all seriousness. "Those poor mermaids. They were a bit underdressed."

Alice laughed. "This doesn't even rate in the same category. It's a Betsy Original, and it's a real mystery. Now that, my dear friends, is excitement."

Annie agreed with her, but after Stella's response, she was torn. What if the rest of the town thought the same way as the older woman? Stella probably had lots of sway in this town. Maybe people wouldn't believe the cross-stitch was an original. After all, Annie had just shown up in town and claimed to find this work up in Gram's attic. Since her grandmother obviously hadn't said a word about it, people might think Annie was pulling a fast one. They might think she'd planted it or, worse, created it herself and tried to pass it off as Gram's. And if some people did believe her, would they help her figure out the identity of the woman, especially with Stella opposed?

She'd really hoped the Hook and Needle Club could help, but not one of them stood up to Stella. Why, she didn't know, but right now, the reason didn't matter. Cutting her losses seemed the best course of action.

Mary Beth reached over and patted Annie's arm. "Promise me you'll bring pictures to the next meeting."

Annie scanned every woman in the circle. Kate's eyes were wide, awaiting her answer. Peggy's cheeks flushed. Gwendolyn's lips curved into an encouraging grin. Stella's brows angled in doubt.

Annie thought long and hard, finally saying, "I'll bring pictures."

～ 7 ～

The fine people of Stony Point might have reason to believe it was okay to pry information from Annie about her plans while she was in town, but she soon found out it was quite a different story uncovering information from them.

To please the ladies of the Hook and Needle Club, she'd taken pictures of the cross-stitch with her digital camera and printed extra copies on her portable printer. One, a close-up of the girl on the porch. Another, a wider view of the piece, including the small scenes. She put a set aside for the next club meeting. She put the other set in her purse, to keep handy in case she needed it, she assured herself. Maybe she could get some answers before the next needlecraft meeting and return with a stronger argument that this was her grandmother's work. How she'd love to prove everyone wrong in the assumption that this might not be a legitimate Betsy Original.

Annie had a list of errands to run, so this would be her chance to show the photo to some of the locals if the opportunity presented itself. Starting a conversation was not the hard part. Figuring out what to do if the person she was talking to suddenly went tight-lipped, now that could be difficult.

She made a few stops before hitting the post office by

midmorning. Annie carried in a care package for her grand-children that contained little doodads she'd collected for them on her road trip from Texas to Maine.

"Not very busy today," Annie commented as the postal worker weighed the box.

"Ayuh. Just missed the Monday morning rush."

"So," Annie glanced at her name badge, "Norma. Have you always lived here?"

"All my life."

"Then you knew my grandmother, Betsy Holden."

"You're Betsy's family?"

"Yes, ma'am."

Norma squinted her eyes. "You should be taller."

Annie suppressed a grin.

"Betsy was tall."

She and her grandmother were about the same height, but Annie wasn't going to correct the woman. Instead, she eased her way into a more personal conversation. "You probably saw my grandmother's needlework over the years."

"Course I did. Pretty handy woman."

"Yes. She always created beautiful scenes. I was wondering if maybe this looks familiar to you." Annie pulled out the close-up and handed it to the woman. "I've been trying to figure out if the young woman featured in the piece is a relative."

Norma squinted harder. "Can't say." She took hold of the glasses hanging over her chest by a long, beaded necklace and placed them on the bridge of her nose. "Doesn't look like any of Betsy's kin."

"That's what I thought. But you know, I can't help but

question why she would stitch a stranger ..." Annie let her voice trail off, hoping the woman would take the bait and fill in any missing details, if there were any.

"Who says she's a stranger?"

Hope rushed through Annie. "So you recognize her?"

"Nope. But if your grandmother knew her, she ain't a stranger. Musta been someone important to her."

Back to square one. Deflated, she reached out to take the photo from the woman when Norma said, "But that barrette looks mighty familiar." She squinted closer. "Had one of those myself when I was a kid."

"So that would have been—?"

Norma gazed across the room, her eyes unfocused as she thought. "Believe I got it at Bascom's Department Store. My mother picked it out, thought it would hold my long hair up nice. When I had hair." A gravelly chuckle sounded in her chest as she patted her short gray hair. "Course, that place closed up a while back."

"So I heard."

"Musta been in the forties sometime. But don't quote me on that. My memory can get fuzzy at times."

"That's more information than I had a few minutes ago. Thanks so much." Annie beamed at the woman as she jotted her name and number on a piece of paper from a notepad she carried in her purse. "If you think of who it might be, give me a call."

"Will do," Norma replied, already busy with another task.

From the less-than-warm responses Annie had received all morning, she considered Norma's revelation a rousing

success. A smile still on her face and a positive feeling inside, she strolled out the door, heading for her last stop of
the morning, an appointment at the bank.

Once inside the Stony Point Savings Bank, she located
the sign-in sheet. With a letter from the attorney, Annie
hoped to get a look at her grandmother's assets.

"I'm John Palmer, president of the bank," a tall, som-
ber, man said as he held out his hand in greeting. So this
was Gwendolyn's husband. How vastly different from
Gwendolyn's sunny and comfortable personality.

"Annie Dawson. I'm hoping we can get my grandmother's banking affairs in order."

"Certainly. Come into my office." He angled a chair
in front of his desk and motioned for her to sit. "Gordon
Procter said he'd taken care of the legal matters of Mrs.
Holden's estate."

"He's the one who advised me to transfer her accounts
into my name."

John pulled a file from one side of his incredibly tidy
desk. "Since he called ahead, I've already started the
paperwork."

The perks of small-town life, Annie mused. She spent
the next half hour reading and signing. At least this was another task she could put behind her.

"Thanks for all your help," she said as she signed the
last page.

"My pleasure." John closed the file and smiled at her.
The smile actually changed his whole countenance, trans-
forming him from dour to friendly. "We're going to be
neighbors now. My wife and I are on the same hill as Grey

Gables. I'm sure you've seen our house."

She thought about it a moment. "The Wedgwood-blue, two-story colonial with white shutters?"

His chest puffed out with pride. "That's the one."

Ah. The well-maintained property. It was almost as if each blade of grass was cut to a meticulous height and trimmed so that not one blade was out of place. A far cry from Grey Gables in its current shabby state. The lawn. She and Wally had put it on the list, hadn't they?

"So I heard. I met Gwendolyn at the Hook and Needle Club. I'm glad we're neighbors," she said—and meant it.

"Gwendolyn mentioned the mystery going on with the needlecraft club, something about a woman in a cross-stitch piece? I haven't seen her this excited in a long time."

Annie pulled out the photo. "Does this young lady look familiar to you?"

John scanned the picture for so long, Annie thought he might have forgotten she was there. "There is something, the curve of the cheekbone maybe, but I can't say for sure I know her."

Annie took back the photo he handed to her. "Thanks, anyway."

"If you need anything, please call." He took a business card and jotted a number on the back. "Our home phone."

She gathered up her things and left the office, her mind on the matter of the cross-stitch. Whom could she ask next? Lost in thought, she stepped out the main entrance, only to collide with a man coming in.

"Whoa, there," he said, grabbing her bag before it spilled to the ground.

Annie looked up to see Ian Butler smiling at her. "Sorry."

"Not a problem."

"I should have been watching where I was going."

"An honest mistake," he said, more than gracious about her bumping into him. "Tell you what, you can make it up to me by joining me for a cup of coffee."

Coffee? With Ian? It was on the tip of her tongue to decline when she remembered the picture of the cross-stitch in her purse. Maybe he could supply some answers. After all, he was the mayor. And he'd offered to help her. "When did you have in mind?"

"How about now? I have to take care of some business first, but I'm headed to The Cup & Saucer in a few minutes."

She nodded, looking forward to talking to him. "I'll go get us a table."

Before going to the diner, Annie dropped her bag at the car, then backtracked down the sidewalk, thinking about her morning. She'd had very few results by showing the photo, but maybe Ian could be a key to unlock more answers. He seemed to keep his finger on the pulse of the town, and he might have insight about the history. Bumping into him might prove to be the best lead she had yet.

As she entered the diner, the bell jingled over head. Since it wasn't quite noon, the restaurant wasn't full yet, so Annie found an empty window table. Peggy was her waitress—again.

"Fancy meeting you here."

"Can't seem to stay away." Annie turned over her mug, indicating she wanted coffee.

"We aim to please," Peggy said as she tapped her pen on

the order pad before asking, "Did you take a picture of the cross-stitch?"

"Yes, just like I said I would."

"Any chance I can see it before Tuesday's meeting?" The devilish gleam in Peggy's eye was hard to miss.

Annie laughed out loud. Obviously, Peggy wanted first dibs. "Do you think that's fair to the others?" she teased.

"Well, I just—" Peggy glanced across the room and whispered, "another time, my boss is watching."

Annie looked around Peggy to see a large man, with his arms crossed over his chest, standing just outside the door to the kitchen, staring in their direction.

"What can I get you?" she said loud enough to carry to the far side of the diner.

Okay, so much for small talk. "A coffee to start. I'm meeting someone."

"One coffee coming up."

Annie idly watched the foot traffic on the sidewalk outside the window. Once summer officially rolled around, Stony Point was like any New England coastal town, bustling with people venturing out to enjoy a day at the shore the rocks or the small beach nearby—or to roam around the Town Square or docks. Some visited Butler's Lighthouse on the jut of land that protected the fishermen's harbor. Vacationers came in all shapes and sizes, from families dressed casually in T-shirts, shorts, and flip-flops, to those in bathing suits and smelling like coconut suntan lotion, or retirees in big hats, enjoying the shops and restaurants. With Independence Day soon upon them, the population would swell over the weekend. After years away, Annie was

happy to see the town still prospered, still lured those looking for a summer getaway.

Peggy returned to fill Annie's cup, and a few minutes
later Ian strode in. He searched the room until Annie waved
him down, then he quickly joined her. "This is what," he
said in way of greeting, "the third or fourth time you've been
here? Looks like you're becoming a regular."

She grimaced. "Third. And a regular isn't the same as a
long-time resident."

He signaled to Peggy, who smiled and headed straight to
the coffee maker. "Does that matter?"

Peggy arrived with Ian's coffee, the coffee she auto-
matically knew to bring him—with one creamer and two
packets of sweetener on the side, even though there were
plenty of both already on the table. She hovered momentarily. "The usual?"

He nodded.

She scribbled on her ticket and asked, "Annie?"

"Coffee's fine for now."

Order taken, Peggy hurried off to another customer.

Annie tilted her head. "And the usual would be?"

"One egg, over easy, smothered in ketchup. Wheat toast,
lightly brushed with strawberry jam. A glass of half ice, half
water, with a lemon slice."

"Well, then, clearly it's evident that you're a regular.
Peggy didn't even have to ask for your order. She has it
memorized."

He grinned sheepishly. "I come here a lot."

Annie wondered why, but didn't pry. She'd learned her
lesson from other townsfolk this morning.

"So that's why you classified yourself somewhere between a regular and a resident?"

"Apparently, I don't fall into either category. I'm related to Betsy and spent summers here as a kid, but just recently came back to town after being away for years."

He chuckled. "The proverbial rock and hard place?"

If only he knew the struggles she'd had since arriving in town. "Exactly."

"So you spent summers here? I'm surprised we never met."

"I ran around with Alice mostly. And my grandmother kept me pretty busy at Grey Gables. She always had some kind of project lined up when I came to visit. The summers went by way too fast."

"Sounds like you enjoyed it."

She smiled. A warm glow enveloped her as she thought about those priceless summers spent with Gram. "Oh, I did. Alice and I had grand adventures when we were kids, discovering every inch of the property and the woods nearby. When we got older, we hung out at the beach. One summer we even got jobs as waitresses at the Grand Avenue Fish House down by the docks." She shook her head and laughed. "That was hard work. I remember limping home some nights."

"When I was a teenager, I worked at the family mill," Ian said with a reminiscent smile. "My dad believed in learning the business from the ground up. Didn't leave much time for hanging out at the beach." He got reflective for a moment then gave Annie a no-nonsense look and asked, "So why does it matter if you're a resident or not?"

"Honestly? I'm trying to find out some answers about my grandmother's past and people around here are ... not exactly forthcoming." Jumping at her chance, she pulled the pictures out of her purse and handed him the glossy photos. "I found a cross-stitch in the attic at Grey Gables. I'm positive my grandmother did the work, but the bigger question I have is, who is the young woman featured on the porch? It's clearly Grey Gables, but I can't get a sense of who she is."

Ian studied the photo. "You're right about the house." He angled the photo right and left to see it in the best light. "It's hard to make out the face of the woman. She's turned away enough that her features are hidden." He looked up at Annie. "Think your grandmother meant to do that?"

Annie paused. She hadn't thought about that. Maybe Gram didn't want anyone to know. And yet she stitched enough of the woman's face to draw you into her secret world, begging her to reveal more.

"That's what I'm trying to figure out. She never stitched people. Always places." She leaned over and pointed out the small scenes surrounding the woman on the second photo. "This is more her style. So I'm completely stumped. I have no idea where these scenes are located or what they mean."

"They could be local," he surmised, squinting to bring the smaller scenes into clearer focus. "I wonder if any of these are original to the town."

"Don't ask me. I sure wouldn't know."

"Which is why you asked a long-time resident?"

"Exactly."

He focused on the photo again. "Do you think this

woman could have been a friend or relative of Betsy's?"

"That's what I intend to find out, but whenever I ask questions, people clam up."

"People in a small town tend to keep to themselves, but I'm not part of that tight-lipped society."

"Even though you're the mayor?"

"Especially so. I want to promote the town, not scare folks away."

"Good policy."

"I've always thought so. But I'm afraid I'm no help. I can't place the woman."

Annie tried to keep her shoulders from slumping. Until this moment, she hadn't realized how much hope she'd hinged on Ian's answer.

"Guess it's back to the drawing board." Resigned, she drank the last of her coffee. Time to head back to Grey Gables and figure out her next strategy. It was times like this she wished Wayne were here to help her figure out this problem. Together, they'd made a great team. Alone, Annie still felt like she was floundering.

"I'll tell you what I can do," Ian said as he stared at the photo. "Let me hang onto this picture. If I study it longer, or ask around, I might be able to figure out where the scenes are located. From there, maybe I can pinpoint a time frame and help you find out who the woman is from that."

"Oh, about the time frame." Annie conveyed her conversation with Norma at the post office.

He whistled low. "I'm afraid that's before my time, but at least we have an idea."

"Ian, I can't tell you how much I appreciate the help.

There's nothing better than having the town mayor on your side."

"That remains to be seen." He held up the photo. "Can I keep this?"

"By all means. I have another copy that I'm going to show the Hook and Needle Club. They're pretty thrilled about this discovery, to say the least."

Ian grinned. "So Mary Beth *needled* you into becoming a member?"

Annie groaned at his pun, but appreciated his attempt at humor. She could see why he had become mayor. He had what it took. He was outgoing and approachable—bad jokes and all.

"Anyway, I'm glad Mary Beth asked me to join them. I enjoy needlecrafts and time spent with new friends. It's just taking a while to get a feel for the group."

"They'll enjoy getting to know you. Give it time. Contrary to what you might think, we aren't entirely exclusive."

"That's what Alice keeps telling me."

"So listen to her." Ian glanced at his watch and pushed back his chair. "Sorry to run, but I need to get back to the office. I'll give you a call if I discover anything."

"Thanks again, Ian."

His eyes held a gleam of fascination. "Trust me, I love this stuff. I've lived in Stony Point all my life, thought I knew everything about everyone. This little mystery is right up my alley."

— 8 —

The afternoon got away from Annie as she took pictures of the cross-stitch. From the full view to individual close-up shots of the scenes, as well as different angles, she intended on blowing them up so the women could see the minute details better. She wished she'd thought of that before giving Ian his copy, but he seemed more than confident that he'd figure out the scenes. Even if he had to use a magnifying glass to make out the finer details.

Before Annie knew it, Boots was meowing for dinner, which reminded her to eat as well. She took a short break, and then she got back to it, going to the one-hour kiosk in the pharmacy adjacent to the mall to print out the pictures.

The clock struck ten when Annie returned home. She'd just placed the photos on the table when she heard a loud creak, like the rusty hinges of the wooden back screen door opening.

"Boots, again," she muttered. The cat had taken to catching her paw under the door and moving it enough that the old, squeaky hinges acted like her own personal doorbell.

"Coming," Annie yelled as she entered the kitchen to let in the spoiled feline.

She opened the back door, then the screen, expecting a streak of fur to charge by. No such luck. Suppressing her annoyance, Annie leaned out the door. "Okay, I'm here.

C'mon in now." She waited a few moments, and still Boots didn't make her grand appearance. Annie stepped out onto the porch. "Where are you?" she called out into the night.

Boots didn't materialize, but in the quiet night, Annie heard a car engine start up and, seconds later, saw headlights brush over the backyard, as if a car had backed down her driveway and turned to continue down the street.

Uneasiness passed over Annie, and she quickly returned to the house, locking the door behind her. She rushed down the hall to the living room, pulled back the drapes at the front window, and caught the sight of red taillights as a car turned onto the cross street. A shudder passed over her. Rubbing her arms, she hurried to the front door, checking the locks. Once she was sure they were secure, she breathed a marginal breath of relief.

She turned away from the door, taking only two steps when Boots tiptoed down the stairs. Annie stopped short, watching in disbelief as the cat sat on the last step to innocently gaze up at her.

The uneasiness returned. If Boots had been upstairs, who had been at her back door? And what was a car doing in her driveway this late at night? She stared at the cat, trying to make sense of things. Try as she might, nothing clicked.

With no answers to her questions, Annie slowly walked back to the kitchen to make a pot of tea, then to the library to find a book. There was no way she'd be sleeping soundly tonight, no matter how hard she tried.

*　*　*　*

The next morning Annie awoke late after only a few hours of sleep. She'd sat on the couch with the lights on, reading and listening for unusual sounds. Finally, at nearly three o'clock in the morning, she'd gone up to bed, not sleeping much better there. Her mind swirled with unwelcome thoughts. Had she really heard the sound? Maybe the wind had blown against the door. Was it all her imagination? But what about the headlights? Was it someone merely turning around after going the wrong way? She didn't have any more answers than the night before, and even her morning coffee hadn't kick-started her yet. Still, she got ready for the Hook and Needle Club meeting, trying to put the unsettling events from the night before out of her mind.

Just before she left, she started having second thoughts about sharing the cross-stitch, but guilt stabbed at her. Hadn't she promised to bring pictures? She'd already placed the photos in her tote but removed them, going back and forth about half a dozen times until she'd made herself crazy by second-guessing herself. Like it or not, she needed help to discover the young woman's identity. She wanted the women on her team. But honestly, Stella's less-than-enthusiastic response gave her pause. Why the older woman's response to the cross-stitch mattered, she couldn't say. But it did.

Annie concluded that Stella just didn't think much of newcomers. She certainly couldn't change the woman's mind if it was set. But could it be something else? Creative jealousy of Betsy, perhaps, that she, Stella, hadn't made a name for herself?

As she drove to town, the uneasiness she felt concerned her. And not just about sharing the pictures. It came from not knowing what the group had in store for her this time. She never knew what they'd say at any given moment. Sometimes they hurt Annie's feelings; other times they inflamed her temper. But judging by their interactions, they did that to each other as well. And if they treated her the same way they treated each other, did that make her one of their own? Perhaps she'd been welcomed into the group more than she realized. The notion warmed her heart and did away with her imminent worries.

As soon as she walked into the shop, Mary Beth raced up to her.

"Did you bring the picture?"

"Yes." She laughed as Mary Beth dogged her steps to the circle of chairs. "And hello to everyone."

The women, all there early as usual, nodded in return, expectation stamped on their faces. Stella refused to look in Annie's direction, but Annie ignored the slight. Annie could play that game as well. She might not like lowering herself that way, but she'd do it for now. Intending to be careful about revealing too much, she removed only the full-view photo from her bag and handed it to Mary Beth.

Mary Beth walked to the wide window where the morning sun poured in and stared at the photo in her hand. After a few moments, Kate joined her.

"What do you think?" she asked as Mary Beth handed the picture to her.

"It looks like Betsy's style."

"Of course it does," Annie confirmed, annoyance creeping into her voice. "I told you it's my grandmother's work."

Kate glanced guiltily at Annie. "We just want to be sure."

Just as Annie suspected. She hadn't even been able to get them to see her side since Stella had convinced the group that this newest find might not be an original. She walked over to the window, gently removing the photo from Kate's grasp. "Does anyone else want to take my word on this, or do you need to see the picture to be sure?"

Peggy set down the piece of gingham she was cutting into different shapes for her quilt, curiosity burning in her eyes. "I'd like to see it."

Annie walked over and handed it to Peggy. She inched closer to Gwendolyn, their heads together.

"Wow. This is something," Peggy murmured.

Gwendolyn nodded. "I've seen Betsy's work, and I have to say this is just as good as anything she's ever done. I could never have done any better."

Pride swelled in Annie. These women may have had their doubts, sown by Stella, but they appreciated the work. "Yes. I believe this is her finest piece."

Mary Beth and Kate joined the other women, and they continued to comment about the cross-stitch. Annie sat, took out her crocheting, and picked up where she'd left off on the blanket. She'd fallen behind, spending all her energy whipping Grey Gables back into shape. Usually crocheting soothed her, but today her nerves were on edge. She chanced a quick peek in Stella's direction, but the woman knitted away, her pace faster than normal, her eyes downcast. She missed a stitch, stopped to fix her mistake, let out an impatient sigh before she continued on. Annie secretly smiled. She guessed Stella wasn't pleased at the group's reaction to the cross-stitch.

The door burst open and Alice rushed in. "Sorry I'm late. I overslept." She stopped short when she saw the women huddled in conversation. "You showed them?"

"Yes."

"And?"

"They like it."

"Like it?" Mary Beth laughed. "That's an understatement. What a wonderful legacy to own a newly discovered Betsy Original."

"Hmph," came from Stella's direction.

Annie refused to respond, even though the woman's stubbornness needled her.

"What are these smaller images around the woman?" Gwendolyn asked as she focused through her bifocals.

"They're different scenes. A storefront, beach, barn, and house."

Peggy squinted. "I wish we could see them better."

"Do you think you could take close-ups of each scene?" Kate asked, her attention still focused on the photo.

"Already ahead of you." Even though she was opening herself up to more criticism, she took out the blown-up shots from her purse.

"We haven't been able to figure out the scenes," Alice said as Annie passed the photos around. "We thought if Annie blew them up, some of you might be able to recognize them."

"If they are local spots, I don't see why not," Gwendolyn looked up and smiled at the store owner. "So much for your summer project idea, Mary Beth. I think we found a new one to keep us busy."

Mary Beth looked through the other photos. "And I'm all for it."

"That's enough." Stella dropped her needles and glared at the group. "We will not stop our project idea to hunt for places that may or may not exist. This is ridiculous. So what if Betsy had a hidden cross-stitch in her attic. She kept it there for a reason and I, for one, say it should go back."

Every woman stared at Stella; her cheeks flushed red and her usually elegant posture tight with tension.

"I think everyone wants to be a part of this mystery," Annie said quietly.

"Not me. Not for one minute."

Confusion creased Mary Beth's brow. "Don't you even want to see it?"

"Not only do I not want to see it, I don't want to discuss this any longer."

"C'mon, Stella," Peggy implored. "We can't ignore it."

Stella shook her head, her features tight as she dug her feet in.

"Then perhaps we should put it away," Gwendolyn suggested as she handed the photos back to Annie.

Silence fell over the room as each woman picked up her needlework. Annie swallowed her disappointment. Had she expected otherwise? Once again, Stella ruined the moment and the women let that happen by not standing up to her. Clearly they were as drawn to the piece as Annie, yet deferred to Stella. As long as Stella was around, she'd get nowhere in identifying the cross-stitch. And as the outsider, she couldn't coax them to do otherwise. Sad, really, but not surprising.

Determined to get the meeting back on track, Gwendolyn asked in general, "What are everyone's plans for the Fourth?"

The three-day weekend would start the summer crush. If years past were any indication, Annie knew there'd be plenty of barbecues, picnics, and loud cherry bomb explosions. A welcome day off from work and firework celebrations on Friday night always drew a crowd, but a chance to enjoy a few days at the beach kept folks here for an extended stay.

"We're open the entire holiday weekend," Peggy groused. "But at least we're closing the diner early on Friday for the big fireworks show."

"I'm working Friday too," Kate sympathized. "And Saturday."

"With all the tourists in town, we need to take advantage of the foot traffic. Sorry, Kate," Mary Beth apologized.

Kate waved her off. "It's not like I had plans anyway. Besides, Vanessa agreed to come in for a few hours both days. I'll be happy to spend time with her. Late Friday afternoon I'll probably help Reverend Wallace out at the church welcoming booth."

"The bank is sponsoring a booth in the park too," said Gwendolyn. "Friday's a big tourist day. We're giving away mugs printed with the bank logo. Not very original, but it makes John happy." She sighed. "I had hoped we could get away from the crowds this weekend, but John takes his bank business seriously. No exotic locales for us."

"Like any of us can afford some place exotic," Peggy sighed wistfully. "Most people find a beach getaway romantic. We have a beautiful beach right here, but do we take advantage of it? No, we spend our time making sure other people enjoy a romantic weekend."

Kate turned to Annie, her eyes shadowed as she said, "Peggy and Wally's ten-year anniversary is next week."

Peggy got a far-away look in her eyes. "Just once, I'd love to go somewhere special. My mom even offered to watch Emily, but Wally's too busy. We need to take advantage of any work that comes his way right now."

Annie watched Kate for a few moments. As much as she tried, Kate couldn't hide the pinched look around her eyes as Peggy spoke about her anniversary. Another wounded soul when it came to love, Annie thought. We should start a new club.

"I'll bet Stella has stories about special vacations. Didn't you travel with your husband?" Peggy asked.

"We did, from time to time, but Seymour was a very busy man."

"Just living in New York City must have been exciting," said Gwendolyn who imagined the life. "The Broadway shows. Central Park. Shopping. John and I traveled there a few years ago for a bank convention. While he met with other bankers, I shopped. We took in a play and had dinner at Tavern on the Green. You must have loved living there, Stella."

"Yes. Yes, wonderful. I was involved with many charitable organizations over the years, sat on the board of one of the art museums. I was responsible for several artists showing their work before reaching critical acclaim."

"And from what I've heard, your husband was quite a catch."

"I suppose so." She shrugged it off, but pride shone in

her eyes. "I was fortunate to marry into the Brickson family. Our families were old friends. We were the same age." She shrugged again, her eyes giving away nothing. "It worked out for everyone."

Alice leaned over to Annie and whispered, "That's the most she's ever shared at one time."

Annie glanced over at Stella, expecting to see the older woman's face softened by fond memories. Instead, Stella remained all business. And Annie couldn't help but wonder why. Maybe Stella's life hadn't been as wonderful as she made it out to be.

"I've always wanted to get down to New York. There's a textile exhibit I want to see," Mary Beth said as she straightened up the fabric-cutting table, getting ready for the teen quilting class later that afternoon. "But business has been good, and I haven't had a chance to get free."

"I told you I'd watch the store," Kate reminded her.

"I know. I just hate to leave."

Kate grinned mischievously. "Mary Beth thinks the store will fall to pieces if she's not here."

"It's certainly not that I don't have faith in you," Mary Beth rushed to assure Kate. "This is my life. I have a hard time walking away."

Peggy rolled her eyes. "You sound like Wally."

Just then the door opened. Two customers came in, and Mary Beth walked over to assist them. Minutes later the phone rang and Kate went to answer it.

"Now you see why she won't leave," Gwendolyn observed.

"And we have a mystery to solve," Alice added, bringing the conversation back to the Betsy Original. "Why would she want to leave? She might miss something."

"I agree," Gwendolyn said. "You know, I'd love to see Betsy's cross-stitch in person."

"Are you sure we can't convince you to bring it to the store?" Kate joined the conversation as she returned from the call.

Annie stole a peek at Stella. If she guessed correctly, those were thunderclouds forming in her eyes. "I don't want to take it from Grey Gables right now." She offered nothing more.

"I wonder what Betsy wanted you to do with it." Peggy fit two pieces of fabric together with a straight pin.

"That's enough for one day," Stella declared as she stuck her needles into the ball of yarn. "Mary Beth, please call Jason."

"So soon? We haven't finished our meeting."

Stella began packing away her supplies. "Yes, right now."

Annie's heart double-tripped. Was Stella leaving because of her? Her intention hadn't been to upset the older woman, even though she couldn't hide her frustration, but obviously any conversation about this new Betsy Original wasn't going to sit well with Stella.

Mary Beth hurried across the room to the phone as Stella stood.

"I'll wait outside." And with that, Stella marched across the hardwood floor and exited the store.

"Wow." Peggy rose with a worried expression and went to the window. "I don't think she's ever done that before."

Great. Annie glanced quizzically at Alice, but Alice merely shrugged.

"Well, my dear," Gwendolyn looked directly across the circle at Annie, a bit of humor wrinkling around her eyes. "You've certainly brought a bit of excitement into our lives."

*   *   *   *

Kate straightened up the how-to book section, the first item on her to-do list in the now-empty shop. The Hook and Needle Club members had all left after the meeting and Mary Beth had gone home for lunch, leaving her alone with her thoughts during this rare break in business.

Rehashing the events of the morning, Kate realized that since Annie had arrived, the fabric of the club had raveled around the edges. The welcome element of change was long overdue. They'd all gotten into a rut, but now, with a mystery to solve, Kate found herself looking forward to meetings that had become dull and predictable. She chuckled out loud. Today certainly wasn't typical. They had the cross-stitch pictures to figure out, and Stella had walked out in a huff. Yes, today had been far from the norm, and Kate found she liked it that way.

Returning to the front counter, she noticed the photos Annie had left beside the cash register. Mary Beth had hogged them, reluctant to put them down until she finally decided to go home for an hour. Now, Kate could finally study the close-up of the young lady.

What was it about her? The air of mystery? The longing that Betsy had so effectively captured? Betsy had truly been an artist. With a twinge in her chest, Kate realized how empty the world seemed without her.

They'd clicked the moment Kate met Betsy right here in A Stitch in Time. She'd been newly married and desperately in need of a hobby, seeing as how Harry had demanded she stay home from work and be a homemaker. Betsy had taken her under her wing and taught her to crochet. You'd think Betsy was her grandmother, the way she'd complimented and cheered Kate on. Through Betsy's prodding and insisting that Kate had talent, Kate discovered she was really good. With her uplifting words or a gentle touch, Betsy always restored Kate's flagging spirits when she needed it most. A special bond had formed, one that Kate would miss always.

Fanning through the photos, Kate focused on the scenes. Something on the edge of her memory stirred, only to slip away as the door opened. Peggy came dashing in, dressed in her work uniform.

"Have you heard from Stella? I've been calling, but Jason says she won't come to the phone."

"I haven't talked to her. Mary Beth tried, but she got Jason as well. Seems she has her mind set on being difficult."

"She's not difficult, she's ... misunderstood."

Kate puffed out an exasperated breath. "When are you going to stop letting Stella influence you?"

"Oh, like you should talk. You always had Betsy to pal around with."

"So Stella is your Betsy?"

Peggy jutted her chin. "Maybe."

"That's so like you to act juvenile."

"And it's like you to take Betsy's side."

"Side for what?"

"This cross-stitch mystery."

"I'm not taking sides. I'm excited about figuring out who the young woman is."

"Even if it upsets Stella?"

"She isn't interested in helping. That's her choice." Kate tidied up the area around the register, straightening the contents of the pencil holder, making sure the business cards lay neatly in the holder, anything to keep busy as she quarreled with Peggy. "Maybe Stella didn't like Betsy. Who knows? Now Betsy's getting all the attention, and Stella doesn't like it."

"That's why we have to be patient with her. She needs us."

"But she always gives us a hard time."

"Because she's lonely."

Kate stared hard at Peggy, convinced by Peggy's insight, though Kate didn't want to admit it. Stella was a member of their club, but she always hovered on the fringes, never revealing the real person or making a true, honest connection with the other women.

"So what do you suggest we do?" Kate noticed Peggy's wary expression and laughed. "What? You were expecting me to disagree?"

"You usually do."

"You have a valid point, so I'm willing to listen."

Obviously surprised at Kate's answer, Peggy took a moment to regroup. "It's pretty clear that Stella doesn't want to help us with the cross-stitch, whether it has anything to do with Betsy or the fact that Annie has recently come to town. Even if she decides to stay away from the club for a while, we need to keep inviting her anyway. To show her we care."

Kate had always thought Stella's actions hinted at a needy soul, but when it came right down to it, Stella was a part of the club. Their friend. "We can do that."

Relief washed over Peggy's features. "I need to get to work. My shift is starting. Promise you'll tell the others."

"I will. Get going before you're late."

"Thanks." Peggy swept out the door, headed for the diner. Kate couldn't help but grin.

Peggy. The human cyclone. Whirling in with her demands, then whirling back out. Yet her heart was always in the right place.

Okay, the least they could do was call Stella regularly. But Stella's reticence wouldn't keep Kate from helping with the mystery. She picked up the photo, trying to catch that elusive wisp of recognition she felt earlier. She focused first on the storefront, then the beach, then the barn.

The barn. She couldn't ignore the kick of adrenaline. Had she seen it before, or was it just like one of the many barns dotting the New England countryside? Before she could decide on an answer, a group of women strolled in.

Hesitantly, Kate returned the picture to the place Mary Beth had left it. Time to get back to work. And try to figure out what niggled her memory.

~ 9 ~

"You had to bring the mystery thread up again, didn't you?" Annie teased later that afternoon as she and Alice took an impromptu walk down to the small beach by Butler's Lighthouse. Even at the end of June, cool sand sifted under her bare feet. Closer to the surf, a chilly mist sent shivers through her body. She slipped on the hoodie she'd wrapped around her waist when she'd left the house.

"Sorry. The gang was enjoying all the talk about Betsy's cross-stitch. I wanted to get the discussion back to it."

"Yeah. And look what happened. Stella stormed out."

"I'm sorry about that, really. I had no idea she'd get so upset."

Annie kicked at some dried seaweed. "Why do you think she's so touchy about it?"

"I don't know if it's a personal thing, your grandmother, or life in general. She hasn't been a very happy person in the years I've known her."

"From the sounds of it, she's had a wonderful life."

Alice shrugged. "Who knows what makes a person happy? I told you she doesn't like to talk about her life in New York all that much. She hardly ever talks about her late husband and never talks about her childhood here. She's one of those people who never truly lets you see the real person inside."

And here Annie had waltzed in, a stranger, rocking the boat that was Stella's life. "I have to admit, I feel kind of guilty. She's been involved in the Hook and Needle Club for years, and in just three meetings I've managed to run her off."

"Don't take it so personally. Like I said, Stella's hard to figure out. She can always find something to be mad about. To each her own."

They walked along in silence for a few moments. Salt from the water tinged the humid air. Seagulls cried out as they dove after fish in the waves. The frothy coastline left behind treasures of the ocean, including myriad shells that were eventually crushed into the sand, alongside rounded stones. Tidal pools of water with sea life swimming inside waited for the next high tide to pull them back into the depths.

Butler's Lighthouse towered in the distance. White washed, silhouetted against the sky, it stood proudly on a peninsula, a beacon to boats on the water as well as a landmark to folks on shore. Annie figured she knew the answer to the question forming in her mind, but she asked anyway. "I take it the lighthouse was named after the illustrious Butler family?"

"One and the same."

What a proud family legacy, Annie thought. She had her own version—in a piece of stitchery. Every family made its own mark. Betsy's had been her amazing cross-stitch flair.

Annie had one thing on her mind. "So is there always so much drama in the Hook and Needle Club?"

"No, you managed to start that all on your own."

"Wonderful. I hope I'm not branded as the troublemaker. I only wanted to make friends."

"I think everyone is secretly glad you showed up. Our routine needed to be shaken up."

Annie wasn't so sure about that but wasn't about to argue the point. Instead, she said, "So tell me about Kate. She's usually quiet."

"She and her husband split up, not long ago. If you met him, you'd know why. He's sweet but gets rough when he drinks. She's still getting used to being on her own."

"Sounds like a theme."

"She'll be fine. She's stronger than she lets on."

"Her crocheted clothing is superb."

"Isn't she talented?" Alice agreed. "All of the jackets she makes are her own design. Your grandmother and I tried to get her to enter her pieces in contests, but she never would. She's really shy about her talent, although Mary Beth has gotten her to display her inventory at the shop.

"Of course, Mary Beth didn't ask if Kate would display her work, per se. She just did it. Said she'd fire her on the spot if Kate made a fuss. The jackets have been displayed ever since. She's made some sales and had requests by customers to make more. So Kate hasn't exactly complained."

"She seems to like talking about Gram."

"Oh, yeah. They were thick as thieves, spending hours plotting a project."

"Gram made it a point to support people with talent and a willingness to learn."

"That's our Kate. She's had a real rough relationship with her husband. He's still making things difficult for her. I think that's why she doesn't like to draw attention to her work, or herself for that matter. She never thinks she's good enough, even though she's about as professional as they come."

"That's too bad. Is her husband around?"

"Yeah, which doesn't help things. Harry is a third-generation Stony Point fisherman. Makes a pretty decent living by fishing, but Kate wants to make her own income and help support their daughter."

"So let me guess, she's another life-long resident too?"

Alice snorted. "Harry, not Kate. Although she's lived here long enough."

"Well, at least I'm not alone. Mary Beth, Kate, and I should form our own club. Outsiders United."

"It won't take that long before everyone forgets you're from Texas. Just watch the y'alls, and things should be great."

"As if it were that easy. I was actually going for that flat accent you Maine people speak with."

"Hmm, so far not so good." Alice veered away from the shore. "What do you say we have a seat while the sun sets before the mosquitoes come out to feast on us?" She headed to a curve in the coastline, leading to a small secluded cove. "Those annoying insects can ruin any party." Inhaling deeply, Alice breathed in the cool ocean air. "I come here all the time to think or get rid of the stress of the day. I love watching the colors change in the sky as the sun sets. It reminds me of some of the cool color choices Kate picks for her clothes. Boy, if I had half her talent ..."

They navigated the cove, staying near the edge of the water. A clump of tall sea grass added a small dash of color to the otherwise sandy terrain. The breeze kicked up, bringing with it the unmistakable scent of rain. Clouds gathered in the south, but not dark or heavy enough to threaten a storm just yet. Annie followed Alice, a nagging sense of déjà vu nudging her as they strolled into the cove. "Did we come here when we were kids?"

"I don't remember. Maybe."

"This place seems so familiar to me."

"Have you been down here since you came back to Grey Gables?"

"No, this is the first chance I've had." Annie rubbed her arms as goose bumps skittered up and down her skin, and the weird sensation grew stronger. "I can't put my finger on it."

Alice dropped down into the sand, the water lapping her toes. "You're still antsy after the club meeting at the shop. Sit. Chill."

Annie arched her brow. "Chill?"

"Whatever. Relax."

Taking one last sweeping glance at the beach around them, Annie was about to sit, when something about the shadow, caused by the sun lowering in the western sky, angled along the sand to the water. Her heart pumped faster. As she backed up to get a wider view, she thought for sure her knees would give out.

"Oh my gosh!"

"What?"

"C'mere." She waved frantically at Alice. How could her friend not see it?

Alice jogged over. "What? What?"

Annie took her by the shoulders and aimed her in the direction she herself had just viewed. Her voice quivered.

"Does that look familiar to you?"

"Sand. Water. Sea grass." Alice shrugged. "I've seen it all before."

"Look again. And then think cross-stitch."

Alice tilted her head one way and the other. Then went totally still. "I can't believe this."

"The way the land curves, along with the water level and the sky color," Annie fanned her hand out over the view. "It's not exact, but it sure looks like the beach scene on the cross-stitch."

"It's been here all along, and I've gotten so accustomed to seeing it, I completely missed it."

"See, we outsiders are good for something."

"Who knew?"

Annie playfully punched her arm. "You know what this means, don't you?"

"We found the first clue." Alice laughed, her expression one of disbelief mingled with awe.

"It makes sense, now that I think about it. This cove isn't very far from Grey Gables. Gram probably came here often."

"We'll have to bring the picture so we can compare, but I have a good feeling about this."

Annie grinned wildly. Things were starting to fall into place, she sensed it. Just as she knew Gram had stitched to-gether the fabric of her life, somehow Annie knew Gram also had hooked her up with these new friends in Stony Point.

Alice shook her head. "I can't wait for the girls to hear about this."

"Our next meeting should be eventful," Annie said,

trying not to visualize what Stella's reaction might be.

Alice gaped at her. "You're going to wait a week to tell everyone?"

Her friend had a point. "Okay, I guess I'm not. I'll call Mary Beth later."

"You bet you will. If we don't tell them right away, we'll never hear the end of it. Trust me, it won't be pretty."

As dark clouds headed in their direction, the wind picked up. It was time to head back to the house in case the sky let loose with a summer rainstorm.

"How about we celebrate our first foray into detective work by letting me whip up something special for dinner?" Annie offered.

"You're on."

They retraced their steps down the beach and returned to Grey Gables. The majestic Victorian stood in stately silence, as if waiting for the women to come inside. For the first time since arriving in Stony Point, the overshadowing sadness Annie harbored for so long began to lighten.

"I wonder if Betsy knew what she was doing when she left that cross-stitch in the attic for you to find."

"Whether she did or not, she left me one last gift." And Annie knew deep in her heart that Gram would be proud. Annie was moving on with her life through the beauty of the cross-stitch.

*   *   *   *

Back in the house, Annie handed Alice the phone, dispatching her with the duty of calling each member of the club. By listening to Alice's end of the conversation, it sounded as if Mary Beth wanted to call an emergency meeting, but Alice talked her out of it since it was so late in the day. Besides, Alice related all the information she had at this point. So for now, the women, except for Stella, who hadn't answered, were ecstatic with the shared news. By the time Alice finished the calls, Annie had dinner on the table. It rained briefly as they shared a victory meal, and then Alice headed home.

Having just put the last clean dinner plate away, Annie finally had a chance to settle down. She'd just set the pot on for tea when the phone rang.

"Mom? You've been a hard woman to reach," LeeAnn teased from the other end of the line.

"I guess that's because I'm a long way from Texas." A wave of contentment washed over Annie. "It's so good to hear your voice."

"Same here. We sure miss you back home."

"Oh, honey, I miss you too. How are you? And the twins?"

"I'm doing great. John and Joanna are growing like weeds. I have them in the church summer camp. They're loving it. And so am I. It gives me a couple hours each day to breathe and get caught up on things around here."

"I'm glad they're enjoying it. Send pictures. And give them a kiss from Gramma."

LeeAnn chuckled. "Will do. So tell me, what have you been up to?"

For the next fifteen minutes, Annie launched into her adventures in Stony Point, from arriving at Grey Gables and meeting her old friend Alice, to the ladies in the Hook and Needle Club.

"Sounds like you're getting pretty settled there, Mom."

"It's not quite like when I was a child and visited Gram, but I'm enjoying myself."

"Have you decided what to do with Grey Gables?"

The teakettle sang as Annie decided to broach the subject. She took hold of the handle, pouring hot water over a peach tea bag. "Not yet. I did hire a handyman for the cosmetic work that needed to be done on the house. Overall, and considering the age, this house is in sound shape."

"So you're keeping it?"

Did she hear censure in her daughter's voice? "Do you think I shouldn't?"

"You live in Texas. How do you expect to keep it up from here?"

"I don't know, but I was thinking about keeping the house in the family. Carrying on the tradition of spending the summer in Maine."

"I don't know … it's awfully far. And Herb has to work."

Annie bit her tongue. She knew better than to prod her stubborn daughter if LeeAnn wasn't ready to make a trip here. She'd have a whole lot more convincing to do before she got results.

"Say, did I tell you I have a Betsy Original on my hands? I found it in the attic. It's amazing work; a young woman sitting on a porch swing here at Grey Gables."

"Really?"

Annie didn't hear any enthusiasm in her daughter's voice, but she continued the conversation anyway as she wandered out to the front porch to sit on a wicker chair, teacup in hand. With the cool evening breeze brushing her skin, Annie explained the woman and the scenes around her; how just this afternoon they'd discovered the beach setting. "I've been doing some detective work to find the identity of the woman, but so far no luck."

"Sounds like fun," LeeAnn said, her tone flat. "So when will you be back?"

Annie paused. She really hadn't thought that far ahead. Then she stopped short. "Wait. Is there something you're not telling me?"

"No. I told you, everything is fine." The tension in her voice said otherwise.

"But?"

Annie heard a rustling sound on the other end. "I miss my mom."

Hearing that her daughter missed her made Annie smile. Even though they hadn't spent a lot of time together in recent months, it softened her heart to know LeeAnn still needed her mother. "And I miss you, honey. Look, you have Herb and the children to take care of. I was rambling around in that big house back home with nothing to look forward to, except seeing you. Now I've made some new friends and I'm finding out things about Gram." She hesitated. "Things about myself."

"You do sound happy," LeeAnn conceded grudgingly.

"I am happy."

LeeAnn sighed. "I guess I didn't realize how much I'd miss you until you weren't here, you know? Does this mean you'll be hanging out in Maine for the entire summer?"

With everything that was going on, Annie couldn't see heading back to Texas any time soon. "Maybe ..."

"Then I guess you'll have to keep me in the loop for now. I want to know how your mystery plays out. So maybe we could talk more often?"

"I would love that," Annie replied, feeling needed by her daughter for the first time in a long time. Too bad she had to be halfway across the country for her daughter to miss her.

She hung up, placing the cordless receiver beside her, and took a sip of her now cool tea. In the distance she heard the surf hitting the shore and seagulls screeching as they dove for food. The sun was nearly set, causing the sky to take on a palette of colors—light blue, deepening to indigo further up in the sky.

After a few more minutes of enjoying the evening, Annie rose, intending to return inside and lock up for the night. As she did, her gaze fell upon the row of impatiens along the house, under the living room windows. Something seemed out of place. Curious, she walked over. Surprise, then concern, filled her when she saw that the plants had been crushed. She checked under another window to find the same results—flowers trampled into the ground.

Gripping the teacup firmly, she walked around the house, checking under all the windows as she went, convincing herself this was nothing to worry about. But just last night she'd thought she'd heard the back door creak and seen headlights out back. This time was no different. Her heart pounded quickly.

Every so often she would come across the displaced plants or trampled flowers. By the time she'd made a full circuit, she was out of breath. What was going on here? As she climbed up the front-porch steps, she noticed a stack of wood neatly placed by the edge of the railing, tucked to the side so no one would trip over it.

Relief overwhelmed her. Wally was still working on the window trim. So that would explain the flower beds. And knowing Wally, he had every intention of fixing the ground under the windows when he finished the job.

Her heart slowed, but she took one last look down the street, searching for anything out of the norm. Other than insects singing their nightly serenade, she was alone. Nothing stirred around her. She was safe.

She had to believe that if she wanted to sleep through the night.

— 10 —

Solving the mystery of the Lady in the Attic, as Annie started to think of the cross-stitch, as well as the strange events at Grey Gables, was put on hold as the entire town got ready for the July Fourth celebration. In her mind, Annie came up with plausible reasons for the night she'd seen the lights and for the trampled flowers. Now, with the holiday here, she would concentrate on town festivities.

Every year Mary Beth set up a table outside the store for children to participate in the construction of patriotic crafts: small flags formed from beads on oversized safety pins; fake sparklers fashioned out of colored straws and sparkly ribbons; and colored sand art, to create the illusion of exploding fireworks.

Usually Kate and Mary Beth took turns manning the table. It was too hot for Stella to sit outside all day, Peggy worked at the diner, and Gwendolyn had other pressing duties planned by her husband. So when Mary Beth asked if Annie would be willing to help, she couldn't refuse. This was her chance to become part of the community. Another step to belonging.

The town put on its Sunday best, at least that's what Annie thought when she arrived downtown. Flags flew in front of homes and businesses. Red, white, and blue banners hung from fences and light posts. In the Town Square, booths were set up for hot dogs and hamburgers, along with souvenirs. Farther down the street, in the park, a late afternoon baseball game between the police force and the volunteer firefighters was scheduled, and later that night the fireworks extravaganza would fill the sky. Vendors hawking everything from miniature American flags to cotton candy and snow cones set up their wares around the park. No one could miss the dunk tank and the first victim, the mayor of Stony Point himself.

Tourists from the area's bed and breakfasts and inns, as well as locals, filled the sidewalks, shops, and restaurants. A buzz of patriotic excitement crackled in the air. Back home in Texas, Annie and Wayne had always volunteered for similar festivities, flavored with a western theme. Since she was in a different town this summer, she couldn't help but become enthralled by the activities special to Stony Point.

"I'm so glad you could make it," Mary Beth told her as she showed up for duty. Dressed in sneakers, denim shorts, and a white T-shirt with fireworks painted in glitter on the front, Annie was ready to do her part.

"I can't believe you found the first clue to our little mystery," Mary Beth said as she straightened out the craft table.

"What mystery?" asked a pretty teenaged girl with long, wavy brown hair and wearing a crocheted beach cover-up of aqua, lined with a bright dandelion yellow. No doubt Kate's handiwork. An even brighter yellow bikini could be seen underneath, evidence that the girl would be hitting the beach later.

Kate stepped beside the girl, putting an arm around her shoulders. "Annie, this is my daughter, Vanessa."

"Hey," Vanessa said.

"Nice to meet you."

"And to answer your question about a mystery, Annie found a Betsy Original up in the attic at Grey Gables. She's been trying to identify a young woman in the piece, so we're all doing a little detective work."

"That's cool."

Annie smiled at the girl, who reminded her of a younger LeeAnn. "We think so."

"Great shirt." Kate pointed to the design glittering in the sunlight as she set up folding chairs. "Did you create that yourself?"

"Yes. Actually, it's free-form. I had a picture in my head and went crazy with fabric paint."

"You do Betsy proud," Mary Beth told her. Then she took a step back and studied Annie's shirt. After a few moments, she snapped her fingers. "You've given me a great idea.

"Kate, run down to the T-shirt shop and see if they have any blank white shirts in all sizes. Sam mentioned he was ordering extra. Tell him to put it on my charge and bring them back here. While she's gone, Annie, gather up some of the fabric paints. With your shirt as advertisement, we can encourage the mothers of the kids who come by for the free crafts to make their own shirts. At a nominal charge, of course."

Annie glanced down at her shirt, then back at Mary Beth's calculating eyes. "You're good."

"Genius is more like it," Kate told her. "She always comes up with fabulous money-making ideas."

Mary Beth shrugged. "It's a gift."

Kate left and Annie finished setting up the craft materials, as well as a table for the T-shirt painting. It was just after noon, and the crowds arrived. Before long, children begged their parents to stop at the beading table. Annie had her hands full supervising the crafts and helping the kids, enjoying every minute of it.

"I see you jumped right in," Alice teased as she joined her an hour later.

Annie glanced at her watch. "Somebody had to start working since you're late."

"Sorry." Alice wouldn't meet her gaze. "Something came up."

"Are you okay?"

"I will be."

There was more to this story, Annie was sure. There always was. But if Alice didn't want to talk in front of the others, Annie wouldn't press her. "Then come get to work. We need an extra pair of hands."

Kate had been able to finagle two dozen shirts from Sam, but they were going quickly, so Mary Beth got on the phone and found two dozen more at a shop the next town over. She took off to retrieve them, leaving the three women to hold down the fort. Kate stayed in the store, ringing up sales from customers. Annie and Alice barely had time to breathe between the rush of excited kids making crafts and the T-shirt sales.

The midday sun lightly burned her skin, but Annie didn't mind. For the first time in months she felt productive and part of a community. The only shadow on the day was when she thought about her grandchildren, wishing they were here to share in the fun. Since that wasn't going to happen, she enjoyed the smiling faces right here in front of her.

Mary Beth returned just in time, since the paint table was running low on shirts. Just as Annie had hoped, the mothers loved the idea of making their own holiday T-shirt. By late afternoon, they'd sold out.

"Another Stony Point tradition," Mary Beth boasted, wiping her hands as if she'd done some major work. "Applause, please."

Laughing, Annie clapped her paint splattered hands together. "At least you're modest about your success."

"Don't encourage her," Alice warned.

"How else do you think I've kept my shop open for so long?" Mary Beth tapped her temple with one finger. "Always thinking."

"No wonder Gram liked you."

"She was a smart cookie too."

Once the crowd thinned, having moved down to the park for food and games, Annie helped the women clean up.

"Mom, can I go now?" Vanessa asked, clearly anxious to make a run for it. "I'm supposed to meet my friends in fifteen minutes."

Kate glanced up at her daughter. "Sure, honey. Make sure you're home by eleven."

"Are you kidding? Everyone is staying out late for the bonfire."

"You know the rules."

"Fine." Vanessa grabbed her beach tote from behind the counter and stomped out of the store.

"I remember that age," Annie quipped as she helped Kate put away the supplies. "Not fondly."

"I look at her sometimes and wonder where my sweet baby girl ran off to."

"She'll be back. Though it'll feel like a few decades from now."

"I don't know if I can hold out that long."

"What doesn't kill you makes you stronger," Alice said from across the room.

"Don't mind her, even though it is true."

Mary Beth came from the back of the store. "Okay, ladies. Let's call it a day."

Alice finished wiping her hands on a paper towel. "Are you saying what I think you're saying?"

"Yes ma'am. It's time to party."

"Let me get my purse." Kate circled around the counter just as the phone rang. She stopped to answer. "A Stitch in Time."

Mary Beth pulled her keys from her pocket. "I think there's a nice big hamburger with my name on it waiting at the park. Are you two going to join me?"

Annie nodded. "Now that you mention it, I am hungry."

They waited by the door for Kate to finish the call. "Ready?" Mary Beth called as she flipped the sign from open to closed, ready to lock up.

Kate hustled outside, preoccupied as she rummaged in her purse for her car keys. Her cheeks were flushed, her motions jerky. "Listen, I need to do something right now. I'll meet you later."

Mary Beth narrowed her eyes. "Everything okay?"

"As okay as usual." Kate pulled a tight smile. "Thanks for your help, Annie. I'll catch up later." That said, she pushed past them to hurry down the sidewalk.

"Was it something we did?" Alice asked.

"No. I believe there's trouble with Harry." Mary Beth bit her lower lip, her expression worried. "I've seen that look on her face enough to know."

When Mary Beth didn't elaborate, Annie chose the smart angle and didn't meddle. Instead she said, "I had a great day, Mary Beth. Exhausting, but great. Are the holidays always so exciting around here?"

"Oh, yes, and you haven't seen anything yet. This is only the beginning. Next there's Labor Day, then Founder's Day and Halloween. And don't forget Thanksgiving and Christmas. I'm going to need all the free help I can get."

Annie regarded the woman who had welcomed her with open arms and reveled in the idea that she might very well be around for all those holidays, included in all the festivities as one of their own.

"The town council always makes sure to draw large crowds," Mary Beth continued. "For the most part, the town derives most of its money during the summer. Lucky for me, I have both tourist and local customers. The locals help me stay open year round, so look out, sister, I'll be calling on you."

Annie's heart swelled. "And I'll be happy to answer."

The women walked down the sidewalk toward the park. From the corner of her eye, Annie spied a Lincoln Continental slowly moving down the street. As she turned to look, the back window facing her was closing.

"That woman really doesn't like me," Annie muttered under her breath. If she was any less obvious, she thought, Stella might as well hit her over the head with a mallet. At this point, it wouldn't hurt any less.

"What?" Alice asked, her attention focused on dodging running kids playing tag.

"Nothing." No point in dragging Alice into this personal ... tug-o'-war between Stella and her. As much as she longed for circumstances to change, she couldn't see Stella making the first move. Annie would have to deal with this her own way.

In the distance she heard the strains from a band warming up amid shouts and laughter. "This is really special, you know? The American traditions. Honor for our country. Back home we celebrate larger than life every year, because, as y'all know, everything is bigger in Texas."

Alice laughed. "We get it. You like Texas."

"But each and every town is special," Mary Beth pointed out. "Stony Point is my home. I've lived here for twenty-five years and wouldn't consider moving anywhere else."

Annie glanced over at Alice. "I'm not going anywhere either."

Alice grinned back. "Then this promises to be an interesting summer. What with the mystery and all."

Once at the park, Mary Beth took off in search of the perfect hamburger. Annie and Alice roamed around, soaking in all the fun and laughter.

"I don't know about you," Alice called over the noise, "but I'm starving."

"Me too. How does a hot dog sound?"

"If it has the works, count me in."

They hunted for a vendor, and after placing their order, ate their fully loaded hot dogs.

"I'm going to regret this later," Alice moaned.

"But it's worth it now."

They moved to a shady spot to enjoy the food. "Last year wasn't great for me. After my husband died, I withdrew," Annie admitted as she watched the hubbub of activity in the park. She inhaled deeply before continuing. "Before Wayne died, he told me to keep enjoying life. I couldn't even imagine it. Now I guess I understand why he said that to me."

"Last year I stayed home too. I couldn't even think about joining in." Alice shook her head. "It's amazing the difference a year makes."

How true, Annie thought. She'd grieved for Wayne. And she never thought she'd be spending the summer in her old stomping grounds, enjoying herself. But life continued on with or without her participation. Wayne and Gram may be gone, but she still had her memories to hold them close. Nothing could ever take them away.

As for Alice, Annie could still see the lingering pain. Everyone healed in their own time.

A trio of boys ran by, jolting Annie from the past to the present. As they called out to each other, she thought of her grandchildren, which gave a little stab to her heart. She made a mental note to call them tomorrow.

The late afternoon wore on. As the sun began to set, Annie watched as groups of families laid down blankets, marking their spots to watch the light show. The merchant booths were closing down, but the food vendors carried on. A lull fell over the park, as if everyone took a collective breather before the main attraction. Once the fireworks show began, spirits would rise and kids would get their second wind. "I should have thought to bring chairs."

"There should be some empty seats in the baseball stands when the game is over. We can watch from there."

"Good. I'm not sure these bones could handle sitting on the hard ground."

"Don't worry, ladies," came a voice from behind them. "I brought extra chairs."

Annie swung around to find Ian Butler smiling at them, his hair still wet from his second dunking in the water tank. "Mr. Mayor."

He nodded. "Mrs. Dawson. Alice."

"Your tourism bureau pulled the people in this year, Ian. I'm impressed."

He shrugged. "A little advertising goes a long way."

"A little?" Alice scoffed. "You pulled out all the stops."

Annie waved her hand out over the park. "I take it this was your idea?"

"Nope, mostly it's tradition. But the tourism bureau put a new spin on it. Looks like it worked."

Alice touched Annie's arm. "Excuse me for a moment. I see someone I need to talk to."

Annie watched Alice weave through the crowd until she disappeared.

Concern laced Ian's tone. "Was it something I said?"

"I have no idea," Annie said, turning back to him.

"The offer of the chairs is still open."

"And I gladly accept."

Ian showed the way to a grouping of chairs at the edge of the park. After Annie sat, he joined her. "I'm glad I ran into you. I have some information about the photo you gave me."

"Really?" Annie scooted to the edge of her seat. With the Fourth of July festivities in full gear, she'd moved thoughts of the cross-stitch in the back of her mind. "What have you learned?"

"I studied all the scenes stitched around the woman. The storefront stood out to me, but I couldn't figure out why. I showed the picture to my father, and the first thing he said was, 'Bascom's. Before it was Bascom's.' He showed me an old family snapshot that I'd seen growing up, and I realized he was right.

"There's no sign over the door in the scene your grandmother stitched, but it has the original federal architectural style from when that block was built. Obviously, it faces a main street. The actual storefront is different, but that's no surprise. Over the years each tenant changes the entrance to reflect its business. Once my father mentioned Bascom's, I went to the library archives and looked in the old town records." He grimaced. "The ones that aren't computerized, I might add."

"Wow. You went to a lot of trouble. I owe you big time."

"And I'll take you up on that, believe me." Ian's expression went from kidding to serious once again as he explained his search. "Lucky for you, the town always kept good records. About twenty years ago, the historical society decided to go through all the files we had stored away and preserve everything. Including old town pictures."

A rush of excitement twisted around in the pit of her

stomach. She could barely speak the words. "So that's good news, right?"

Ian nodded. "I believe this is the building that used to be Bascom's Department Store. It currently houses Dress to Impress."

"So my grandmother stitched a store that was once in this town." She immediately recounted the discovery of the beach scene. "Ian, I'll bet the two remaining scenes are right in this same area."

"I would think so."

This was better than she'd dare to hope. "Did you come up with a date?"

"The store before Bascom's was open in the 1920s until the early '40s, when it changed owners and became Bascom's."

"That coincides with what Norma at the post office told me." She beamed at Ian. "Another real clue."

"Surprised?"

"That you found something? Not at all. Everyone says you know all about this town. Why do you think I asked the expert?"

"I don't know about being an expert, but I do love this town. And I know where to look for information."

Without his help, and Alice's, she'd never have gotten this far. Each step brought her closer to discovering the identity of the young lady. Another step forward in her personal quest. "Thanks so much, Ian. I really mean it."

"So what's your next plan of action?"

"I don't know. I guess I'll figure out who lived in town at that time, see if they're still around, or alive even, and ask more questions. Do you think your Dad might know anyone else?"

"I asked, but he didn't seem too confident. You'll have to continue asking around."

"And we both know how well that goes."

Ian chuckled. "Tell people I sent you. You might get better results."

"Deal." Annie thought for a moment. "I guess this means we'll be going back to The Cup & Saucer soon."

"Why's that?"

"I owe you a cup of coffee and a slice of pie for all your help."

"I never turn down the offer of pie."

During the conversation, the sun had set. The street lamps were dimly lit, casting an inviting atmosphere for the fireworks show. Children ran about as their parents settled on blankets or pulled out lawn chairs to get ready for the upcoming display of sound and color.

Annie settled back, soaking in the small-town charm. Right now, sitting and observing families and friends enjoy the holiday outing, she felt at ease. Oh, she missed LeeAnn and the grandchildren, her home and garden, even her town, but something was changing for her. Something good. And she didn't want to leave Stony Point until she figured out what that was.

She was making friends. Alice, Mary Beth, and Kate. Even Ian.

Finally, she felt as if she was fitting in.

She had a town to discover and a mystery to solve.

The night wrapped her in promise. And when the dark

sky burst into bright flashes of red, blue, green, and gold, children cried out oohs and aahs with each explosion. Annie smiled and drank it all in.

Until a funny tingling started at the base of her neck. She looked around, wondering if someone was approaching her. But everyone around her was entranced by the fireworks. They weren't the least bit interested in Annie.

Minutes passed, but not her hyper-awareness. The creepy feeling continued, as though someone was watching her. She glanced at Ian, but he too was watching one explosion after another in the sky. Standing, she stretched her legs, taking the opportunity to turn around and check out the area around her. Again, nothing out of the ordinary for an extraordinary night.

Okay, too much excitement for one day, she thought. No need to be paranoid. Turning her attention back to the grand finale, she couldn't help but think that things were going along fine—weren't they? And if they were, why did she get the feeling that something explosive was about to happen?

~ 11 ~

Annie awoke the next morning after a long night of peculiar dreams. Had someone been watching her? Still, there had been so many people in the park, what had she expected? The uneasy feeling had stayed with her as she drove home. She tried convincing herself that the car behind her was not following her, especially when it turned off before she arrived at her street. Once in the driveway, she sat in the car for a few minutes, her breathing tight, scanning the dark road behind her. When no car passed by, she finally got out of the car and hurried into the house.

Should she tell someone about this? She thought about calling Alice, but really, what would she say? Other than her suspicions that things seemed off, she had no proof that anyone was actually following her or sneaking around the house. This was more than she bargained for when she came back to Grey Gables.

Shaking it off, she made a pot of coffee, mentally planning her day. Spying the hardcover journal lying on the counter, she grabbed it and a pen before sitting at the kitchen table. Sometime during her sleepless night, she'd come up with the notion to keep a log of everything that had transpired so far. LeeAnn and the twins had given her this fancy journal before she left, making her promise to record every detail of her trip. At this point, she had plenty to write about.

Before Annie got to work penning her entry, Boots sashayed around her ankles, butting her head against Annie's leg, clearly kissing up in hopes of scoring more crunchy food. "You just ate," Annie scolded, only to be met with an irritable meow.

Chuckling, Annie jotted down the date she arrived at Grey Gables. She chronicled her impressions of the Victorian house, then listed subsequent events: following Boots to the attic and finding the large, covered frame, renewing her friendship with Alice and her encouragement to help find the identity of the young woman in the cross-stitch, and noting Ian's help. The words flowed freely, including her impressions of meeting the members of the Hook and Needle Club and drawing them into the mystery. After all that, she included a section on how solving this mystery had taken on personal importance. Finally, she wrote in dark, bold letters: CLUES.

Beach scene. Cove, compared to stitched scene, a match. The landscape hasn't changed much and the essence of the scene is still the same; evening sun casting shadows on the cove. Proximity to Grey Gables confirms find.

Bascom's. Storefront scene, ascertained by Ian. Or rather, Ian's father. Basic architecture of the building unchanged, the storefront currently different than in cross-stitch because of a new tenant.

Two down, two to go. Still, she couldn't deny the thrill of the hunt. And she had to admit, she was getting pretty good at this. She brought the pen to her teeth, biting on the end as she pondered the remaining scenes. Where to look next?

She was about to call Alice for advice when the phone

rang. When she heard Joanna's voice, she couldn't contain a big grin.

"Hi, Grammy. When are you coming home?"

"I'm not sure, sweetie. There's still a lot to be done around the house."

"Mama showed me a picture. The house is big."

To a five year old, the rambling Victorian probably seemed like a fairy-tale castle. It had to Annie at that age. "You'd love it, Joanna. There are lots of places to play hide-'n'-seek. And I'm sure there's a tea set around here somewhere to play with."

"Are there bugs? John scared me with a big, black one yesterday. I don't like bugs."

"No bugs, just a bossy house cat." Annie grinned, picturing her all-boy grandson terrorizing his sister. "Don't worry. I would never let anything happen to you."

"Mama says we can't come see you until you get home."

Hmm. Her daughter had been saying a bit too much. "Why don't you put your mother on the phone?"

"Okay. Love you."

"Love you too."

Seconds later, LeeAnn's voice came over the line. "How's the absentee grandmother doing today?"

"Fine." She ratcheted up her mother tone. "Putting Joanna on the phone won't get me home sooner. The divide-and-conquer tactic never worked with your dad and me when you were a child. It won't work now."

Properly chided, LeeAnn sighed with guilt. "It was worth a try."

"Please don't do it again." Point made, her voice softened.

"I miss you all, but I have to finish things here."

"How is the restoration going?"

Annie went into detail about Grey Gables, what they'd already done and what remained on the to-do list.

"And the cross-stitch?"

"We found another clue." Delight rang in Annie's tone as she relayed the newest info to her daughter. "Only two scenes left. In fact, I'm looking at my clue list right now, considering where to focus next."

"Mom, don't you think you're getting carried away?"

Carried away? "What makes you say that?"

"You're all gaga over a stitching on a piece of material."

"It's important to me right now. And besides, your great-grandmother did the cross-stitch. It's one of a kind."

"It's all you talk about, like you're obsessed or something."

Obsessed? "Do I sound that bad?"

"Well, maybe not that bad, but close. I think you need to forget about it and come home."

Go home? Not yet. Not while she was still searching for the Lady in the Betsy Original.

They chatted a few more minutes before LeeAnn had to referee what sounded like a shouting match. Annie heard the squabbling children in the background and smiled, missing them more than ever.

Once off the phone, in the quiet kitchen, Annie scanned her list. Was she obsessed? She hadn't really thought so, but if you were being obsessive, did you know it? Rubbing her temple, she tried to ease a headache.

Maybe she was obsessive, because as she looked at her list of clues, she knew she couldn't give up now. Didn't want to. Not with only two clues left to solve, bringing them closer to the identity of the young woman in the cross-stitch.

Which would bring her full circle.

She'd come to Grey Gables to put her grandmother's affairs in order, only to find herself completely embroiled in a mystery. Between finding that part of herself she thought she'd lost after her husband died and uncovering the identity of the young woman, maybe Annie would find peace. At least she hoped so.

Shaking off her far-fetched thoughts, she refocused on the task at hand. Since Annie didn't know the local area around Stony Point as intimately as she wished, she knew she'd have to rely on her next-best source of information, the Hook and Needle Club. Weren't the ladies absolutely champing at the bit to be more involved? Besides, Annie needed them for support and for their knowledge. And to help her uncover this mystery so her daughter would stop thinking Annie had lost her marbles.

* * * *

By Tuesday morning, the women of the Hook and Needle Club were in a tizzy about the beach clue, bombarding Annie with questions. The main one: Was she sure it was the right place?

"Yes," Annie answered for the third time. "I brought the blown-up picture to the cove to compare. It looks remarkably like the stitched scene. And yes, when Alice gets here, she can confirm the find."

Mary Beth sat perched on the edge of her seat, her

laser-beam gaze aimed directly at Annie. "Give me all the details."

Nestled in a chair in the circle of friends, Annie made herself comfortable and continued. "We happened to be at the beach at the right time, early evening, as the sun was sinking. The long shadows and the way the sand and water met, it was perfect. Not one-hundred percent like the cross-stitch, but close enough that if you saw it for yourselves, you'd agree."

"I can't believe I missed being there," Mary Beth grumbled.

"It wasn't like we found it without you on purpose. It just happened," Annie consoled her friend, trying not to chuckle out loud at Mary Beth's disgruntled pout. "When I was younger and tagged along on nature walks, my grand-mother would bring a sketch pad in case she came upon a setting that caught her eye, quickly fleshing out a scene so she wouldn't forget. We came home from a walk more than once with a rendering or two, then we'd sit down and come up with the colors from memories as well as her notes. Before I knew it, my grandmother would transfer her vision to cloth. She amazed me every time."

"A clue answered," Gwendolyn marveled. "And so quickly."

Finally, after confirming all the questions, she readied herself to surprise them with yet another doozy. With a sly smile she said, "Not just one. Two."

The room went silent.

"Two?" Peggy repeated.

"That's right."

"What? When?" Gwendolyn sputtered.

Annie chuckled at Gwendolyn's reaction. "I ran into Ian Butler a few days before the July Fourth celebration and mentioned our little mystery. He was intrigued, especially when I showed him a photo of the cross-stitch. When I ran into him at the park this weekend, he told me he believed the storefront scene was most likely Bascom's, before it was Bascom's."

Kate jumped up and looked out the window, down the street toward the building in question. Within seconds Mary Beth, Peggy, and Gwendolyn crossed to stand before the glass with her. If it hadn't been for a worried customer entering the store—wondering if they were tracking a thief or something—the four women would have stood there longer, staring down Main Street.

Peggy returned to the circle of chairs first, followed by the others. "I can't believe he beat us in uncovering one of the clues. He's not even a member of the Hook and Needle Club."

"We could make him an honorary member," Gwendolyn quipped. "But I doubt he'd come to our meetings."

Annie laughed. "I think he has his hands full being mayor."

"Which would explain how he determined the location of the storefront. He has access to all kinds of town history."

"That and his father has a good memory. Apparently, he recognized the store. Ian said his dad has an old snapshot with that building in the background. The buildings on that block were constructed before the town grew and expanded, making way for Main Street as we know it. Bascom's had a fancy storefront built when it opened, and it stayed that way for years, until Dress to Impress renovated and modernized the look."

"Makes sense." Gwendolyn resumed her knitting. "The Butler family has a lot of history in this town. And they all live long, which would explain Thomas Butler's knowledge."

"And that made me wonder if there are any other older residents in town who might recognize the two remaining scenes." Annie scanned the group. "Surely y'all might know someone."

Gwendolyn dropped the half-finished scarf to her lap. "Many of Betsy's contemporaries have passed on. There might be some folks living in the Senior Center we could ask. I'll check next time I visit."

"And there's Stella," Peggy reminded them.

Annie glanced at her watch. "Where is Stella anyway? Every time I've come to a Tuesday meeting, she's already seated in her chair, working away on that sweater."

Mary Beth finished with the customer and joined them. "I think she's taking a break for a while."

Annie's heart squeezed tight. "Oh, dear. It's my fault, isn't it?"

"She said some things had come up, and she'd be staying home for a few weeks."

"What could she possibly have going on?" Peggy asked with concern. "In all the time she's been a member, she's never missed a Tuesday meeting. She's never had anything come up before."

"Maybe she has plans with other friends," Gwendolyn supposed, her tone less than convinced. "Every once in a while she tries to revive her idea of starting some sort of a cultural center in town. Not that we need one, after all. What would we showcase? Lobster pots? Although, you can rehab them and use them for lovely flower planters. I happen to have two on my back patio and—"

"Gwendolyn." Mary Beth interrupted the odd segue.

Annie noticed that Gwendolyn went off on a tangent whenever the conversation turned a bit tense. Usually whenever Stella was involved. Her meanderings always lifted the general mood of the group. It might come across as silly, but Annie suspected the woman knew exactly what she was doing.

Gwendolyn pulled herself back to her original thought. "Anyway, Stella has always wanted a cultural presence here. Most likely because of her work in New York. Perhaps she's decided to meet with members of the Historical Society to talk to them about her ideas."

"Now that makes sense," Mary Beth agreed. "She touches base with them from time to time."

"I saw her driver, Jason, at Magruder's this morning," Kate told them as she fitted one of her crocheted jackets to the dress mannequin. "He said 'hi' but seemed distracted, like he was in a hurry or something. Stella was nowhere to be found."

The door opened and Alice sauntered in.

Peggy's hand flew to her throat. "Maybe Stella's sick."

"Don't think so." Alice strode to the circle. "Sorry I'm late. I had an appointment earlier." She dropped her purse and tote bag before sinking into one of the chairs. "I saw Stella at The Cup & Saucer. She was chatting away with a table full of women, one of whom I'm sure is from the

Historical Society. So I'd say she's fine."

Peggy's brows arched. "I never believed she actually had other friends besides us. And she's at the diner, on my day off." She rifled through her purse and pulled out her cell phone. "I'll find out what's going on."

"The rumor mill at its finest," Alice joked.

"She does socialize," Gwendolyn said. "It's good she has friends besides us. They get her out of the house on other days of the week."

"Yes, but are they her real friends?" Peggy challenged, a touch of hurt lacing her voice, as she punched in a number.

Gwendolyn's eyes widened in concern. "I hadn't thought about that."

Kate walked around the mannequin to check the back of the garment. "We don't see her all the time, Peggy, but she knows we consider her our real friend."

"But she never talks about anyone else, so I have to wonder." Peggy stopped as her call went through. "Hi, Lisa. Hey, quick question. What is Stella up to over there?" She paced the small area around the counter as she listened.

Mary Beth arranged a bin of sale yarn on a table near the door. "There's no stopping her when Stella's got an idea in her head. And she's decided to stay away."

Alice pulled her unfinished cross-stitch cloth out of her tote, resting it on her lap as she threaded a needle with green floss. "Have you spoken to her recently?"

Mary Beth didn't answer at first. Her eyes flitted to Annie. She squirmed as she toyed with a skein of yarn. "Just yesterday. She told me she wouldn't be returning until after we'd solved our silly little mystery."

"I knew it." Annie dropped her crochet in her tote. "This *is* my fault."

"She's a grown woman," Gwendolyn said. "She can make her own decisions. If she doesn't want to be here, we can't make her."

"She's the one missing out." Kate gazed at Stella's empty chair.

Annie didn't know what to think. Of course Stella wasn't here. She'd made no secret of the fact that she wasn't interested in anything to do with the cross-stitch, or with Annie for that matter. The other women's enthusiasm about the mystery had clouded Annie's better judgment about involving them without concern for Stella's wishes. Stella was truly a part of this group, just as the women had testified. More so than Annie. Yet Annie had obviously upset Stella, causing her to stay away. Annie had never intentionally hurt someone before, and she hated that she'd done so now.

"I feel awful," she blurted.

"Don't," Peggy replied with a dramatic sigh as she pressed the end button on her phone and plopped down in her chair. "Okay, here's the scoop. Stella is with some of the women from the Historical Society, brainstorming ideas about how to get a cultural center up and running. Apparently Liz Booth, president of the Historical Society, wants to form some kind of merger between the cultural and historical clubs. I didn't even know Stony Point had a cultural club."

"That would be us," Alice informed her.

"Anyway, sounds like Stella and Liz have been discussing the idea for a while now. With some space coming empty on the ground floor of the Walker Building, they want to formalize plans." She glanced around the circle, eyes wounded. "I understand that she wants to get things rolling, but why didn't she tell us? Or even include us?"

Kate walked over, sat on the arm of the chair, and placed her arm around Peggy. "She has dreams, too, just like all of us. It's time we let her fulfill them her way."

"Maybe we're her creative go-to people," Gwendolyn speculated. "But she needs practical people to help her get the center open. People with connections we don't have."

Peggy glared at Annie. "Stella let the idea for this cultural center drop until you came to town."

Kate squeezed Peggy's shoulders. "You can't blame the timing on Annie. Obviously Stella doesn't confer with us on every part of her life. She kept this from us for a reason."

Peggy slumped. "I can't believe she'd do that."

"We can't force Stella to pick," Mary Beth advised. "Right now she wants to be involved with another pet project. All we can do is support her if she asks."

"And if she doesn't?" Peggy leaned away from Kate. "If she thinks we've betrayed her somehow?"

"Then she'd be wrong." Kate rose, returning to the mannequin. "We'll have to keep in contact with her. Keep connected. We'll take turns calling her every day."

Everyone agreed, committing to stay in touch with Stella daily. They may not have said it out loud, but Annie felt like she was the catalyst in Stella's decision to abandon the group. Stella may not like her, but Annie shouldn't have made her uncomfortable to the point of leaving, creating a gaping hole in a room full of old friends.

"Listen," she told the group. "I can finish figuring out this mystery on my own time. If we don't talk about it, Stella can come back here, and things will go back to normal, right? I'll even stay away if it helps. I don't want to be the cause of dissension in the club." While she didn't like being the cause of Stella leaving, she liked even less the thought of leaving her newly won friends. She lifted her chin confidently, despite her feelings to the contrary.

"Besides, I have plenty of work to do at Grey Gables. Sprucing up that place will probably take me until the end of the summer anyway. Wally is doing a great job, but if I pitch in more, we may finish ahead of schedule."

"Then what?" Alice asked.

Annie faltered momentarily before pasting on a self-assured smile. "I guess I go back to Texas."

The women in the group eyed one another, a silent form of communication that came from years of knowing one another. As much as it intrigued Annie, it also proved she was still an outsider.

She pushed away the profound ache, believing she was doing the right thing for everyone.

Mary Beth finally nodded, understanding the general consensus of the group. "Stella made her choice, Annie, but we still want to help you find out what the cross-stitch means. Betsy was our friend, too. And now you. Please, don't shut us out."

Annie considered this quietly. Kate hovered beside the mannequin, fussing with the display while darting frequent glances her way. Gwendolyn stopped knitting, her needles idle as she awaited the answer. Alice stared right at her, an amused grin tilting her lips. Peggy narrowed her eyes. Annie wasn't sure what that meant.

But she did know that in the short time she'd been here, these ladies had, indeed, become her friends.

"Okay, I'll stay in the club. As long as we agree not to discuss the cross-stitch in front of Stella any longer. That way, maybe she'll come back."

Mary Beth's face brightened. "Deal."

"But if we can't talk about it here, then where?" Kate asked. "This has always been where we talk about our works in progress and other needlecraft ideas. And the Betsy Original is definitely a topic of conversation. How on earth do we talk around it when Stella is here?"

"We find a way, Kate." Peggy lifted her chin in determination. "I'm all for Stella coming back, and if that means no Betsy Original talk, then we save that for other times when we're together without Stella."

"That would work," Gwendolyn agreed.

"Then it's settled," Peggy proclaimed, ever loyal to Stella. "We make this a 'non-Betsy Original zone' for Stella."

"So when can we talk about Betsy's work?" Kate asked, her brows pinched like a headache was coming on.

Alice shared a knowing look with Mary Beth, who grinned wickedly. "We know just the right time."

"Really?" Annie asked, curious of the suspicious exchange between her two friends. "What does that mean?"

"Road trip," Alice and Mary Beth sang out in unison.

⌐ 12 ⌐

Road trip unanimously decided upon, Kate suggested looking for the barn. She held one of the pictures in her hand. "I've been studying this one, and something seems familiar to me, but I can't quite put my finger on it." She held her forefinger and thumb an inch apart. "It's this close."

"Since the other two scenes are right here in the area," Mary Beth concluded, "it would make sense that the other two are also here in Betsy's stomping grounds."

Gwen had alternative ideas about the location and wanted to check them out before setting out on their hunt. Since Sunday was the first day they were all free at the same time, they agreed to meet at the shop at eleven. A Stitch in Time would be closed for the day, and Peggy's shift at the diner didn't start until later.

Meanwhile, before the road trip, Annie had things to take care of at Grey Gables. Wally had finished the outside work and was ready to tackle the inside of the house. Annie decided to take the rest of the week selecting paint colors to freshen up the living room and kitchen. Not sure what direction she wanted the decorating to go, she invited Alice over on Friday afternoon to help her pick colors.

"I asked you here, Ms. Divine Décor, because I need a professional opinion." Annie set two steaming coffee mugs on the kitchen table, a stack of paint chips in front of them.

"No pressure, I assume?"

"None whatsoever. I need some friendly advice here."

Alice scooted her chair back to seriously assess the kitchen. "Any idea what look you're going for?"

"I thought maybe retro Grey Gables. Bring back the theme I remember from when I was a kid."

"Your grandmother had a theme?"

"Her not having a theme was her theme. She'd get an urge to paint, and she'd paint. Then add wallpaper or a border. As you can see, not much matches in this room anymore. Or any other room in this house, for that matter."

Alice settled in, all business. "Hmm. Sounds like eclectic country. What do you remember from when you visited?"

"Sunny yellow walls. Calico curtains. Shiny wood floor."

"It's going to take plenty of work, but we can start by stripping the wallpaper before we repaint. I'm sure Wally can buff the floor to its original state. And the curtains ... we'll come up with something. After all, we do know a few people who are a whiz at sewing."

They chatted about redoing the kitchen for a few minutes before Annie asked, "What have you been up to?"

"Booking and preparing for Divine Décor and Princessa parties." Alice poured sweetener in her mug. "The summer can get pretty busy. I rent a space downtown with my top hostess a couple nights a week. We target tourists and get them to stop in. It's been a hit, and the regulars like the perks of always having a party booked. It's a win-win."

"Good for you. I love seeing successful businesswomen."

"Wish you were working again?"

"Not right now. I've been too busy around here to miss the hectic grind of an everyday job. Although, I loved being a part of something, like I was at the dealership. Owning the business gave me a sense of purpose."

"And now?"

"Now I have Grey Gables, the Hook and Needle Club, and the cross-stitch mystery to think about. That's more than enough to fill the hours in the day."

"Okay, then."

Annie stared into her coffee and blew out a worried sigh.

"What's up with you?" Alice laid down the spoon she'd been stirring her coffee with. "You asked me over here for more than just color choices, didn't you?"

"You got me." She glanced at Alice. "I'm feeling awful about this Stella thing. I saw her at the post office yesterday. Of course, I made things worse by trying to talk to her. She was polite ... but distant."

"I have to say, I love Stella, but she can be pretty hard at times. And she can be stubborn once she gets an idea in her head."

"And right now her idea is that she wants no part of the mystery. Because of me." Annie's heart sank. "Why doesn't she like me?"

"I think that's a bit strong. She just gets a notion in her head from time to time and runs with it. Maybe she sees you as a threat to her pet project? I don't know. All she sees is that you came into town, joined the Hook and Needle Club, and drew the girls right into a mystery. A mystery that has gotten a lot more attention than a possible, in-the-works cultural center."

"I still feel guilty."

"Annie, don't let Stella have that power over you. You're a part of the club, and we're happy to have you. Stella needs to accept the changes."

Annie rose and walked to the window, staring out at the backyard. The grass was thriving now that it had been fertilized and watered daily. Late azaleas, lady slippers, and petunias accented the yard with color—plums, pinks, and fuchsias. In a few weeks, Annie planned to go berry picking and try out Gram's old pie recipes.

Turning, she faced Alice, resting her hip against the counter. "When I came back here, I only meant to tie up Gram's affairs and quickly decide what to do with the house. I never imagined I'd make friends so quickly. The Hook and Needle Club accepted me with open arms. And I have to admit, I really needed that. My life in Texas had become ... monotonous. One day sort of merged into the other, and I'd lost interest in most everything. Even though I have the grandkids, it's different. Now," she swept her arms open, "with this place, I look forward to every day as a new adventure. The Betsy Original has had my mind occupied with 'who?' and 'what?' since the first day I saw it. I won't be able to leave here until I know the whole story behind it."

"That's good, because we don't want you to leave."

Annie crossed the room and sat again. "You don't think I'm obsessing, do you?"

"Why would you ask that?"

"My daughter mentioned it."

"Why on earth would she think that?"

"Well, I read her my list of clues—"

"You've made a list?"

"Sure. I'm detail oriented."

Alice chuckled. "Go on."

"And she mentioned that I'd really let this thing get under my skin."

"You have." Alice took a sip of her coffee. "In a good way." She set down her mug, all seriousness now. "Look, I haven't seen the club this single-minded in a long time. Not since Stella promised us all a trip to New York, and she bailed on us last minute. This is bigger than our yearly project. And we all want to be involved."

"Almost everyone."

"I know you think you've pushed Stella away, but she gets prickly about new things all the time. The girls want this, need this, maybe. We're all tied to this town, not in a bad way, but because we love it here. But from time to time people get in a rut. That's where we've been with the Hook and Needle Club. We needed a shake-up. You and Betsy have given us that."

"So I'm not acting too crazy about the cross-stitch, am I?"

"No. Not any more than Mary Beth. It's all she talks about."

"I really should let her come over and see the real thing. I don't know why I'm hesitating. Once the others see it ... I don't know, it's like it becomes a piece of history, not just a gift from my grandmother. I'm not ready to share it."

"But you will eventually?"

"Yeah. Just let me be selfish a little longer."

"I think the girls can understand that." Alice's grin

turned cagey. "It makes them more determined to find out who our mystery woman is."

"We will find out, won't we?"

"Count on it. Once the Hook and Needle Club set our collective minds together, there's no stopping us."

*   *   *   *

On Sunday morning, the six women met on the deserted sidewalk outside the shop with to-go coffee cups in hand, courtesy of Annie. She'd stopped at the coffee shop on the way to meet the girls, treating them all to coffee. It was the least she could do since they'd offered to go along with this hunt on their day off.

Gwendolyn was the last to arrive, map in hand. "Sorry I'm late. John wasn't very happy that I left as soon as Sunday service ended, instead of mingling like we always do. But I assured him Reverend Wallace wouldn't notice." Excitement flushed her cheeks. "I couldn't sleep last night. When was the last time we did something this spontaneous?"

"When we went on that yarn run," Kate recalled. "We hit every yarn store between here and Portland. Then we stopped for lunch at a pricey restaurant."

"We should do this more often." Peggy tugged her purse strap up her arm. Her mood seemed to have lightened since the other day. "Road trips are like mini-vacations. I've been ready since Tuesday."

Alice winked at Annie. "I told you."

"You did."

Peggy scanned the parking spaces. "So who's driving?"

"I am," Mary Beth replied. "My SUV can seat us all comfortably. Let's pile in and get this show on the road."

"Before we go, I want a group picture for my daughter. Since I've talked nonstop about the town and you ladies, she wants me to send pictures." Annie waved them to the window with the stenciled store name—A Stitch in Time—boldly centered behind them. As everyone bunched together and smiled, Annie took the shot. She lowered the camera to check the view box. "Perfect. Now, let's make tracks."

"Where to, Gwendolyn?" Mary Beth asked as the vehicle doors closed and she put the SUV in gear.

"I went to the Senior Center the other day and asked around. General consensus was to head inland. If we forgo the highway and stay on the rural roads, we stand a better chance of finding some old barns." She pulled a map from her bag. "I jotted down the route to an area of farmland I remember driving by once with John. I'm hoping we have success there."

"I think my grandmother had some cousins who lived in that direction. She might have visited and gotten inspiration for the cross-stitch. Seems as good a place as any to start."

With that plan in mind, the women headed out of town. Between the chatter and laughter, Annie's heart swelled. This was a good thing they were doing. For her, it meant forging new friendships. For the others, solidifying the relationships that already existed. In light of the anticipation on each face, this was going to be a successful day, whether they discovered anything or not. Actually finding the barn would be icing on the cake.

Annie had never really spent much time outside of

Stony Point, so she enjoyed the sights as much as the lively conversation.

Summer had dressed herself in a glorious palette of color; the variegated greens of sweet summer grass and darker leaves of towering maples. Wild daisies and black-eyed Susans dotted the sides of the road. A bright blue sky held few fluffy clouds. Since viewing the cross-stitch and talking about her grandmother's work, Annie found herself looking at color differently—with more of an artist's eye, like Gram. Since coming to Maine, everyday life became less mundane and filled with promise.

As they headed to less populated areas, the land grew more hilly, but no less beautiful. The air grew crisper as they headed into woody areas. Within an hour they met with longer stretches of uninhabited woodland without passing farm houses.

"I think maybe we've come too far," Annie told Mary Beth. "I can't imagine my grandmother traveling this far away from Stony Point, even if she had relatives out this way."

"We should find the farms soon," Gwendolyn muttered as she fussed with the map and notes she'd brought along.

Off the heavily traveled roads, they eventually found the area of farmland that Gwendolyn had directed Mary Beth to, but they grew disheartened when none of the barns they came across resembled the one in the cross-stitch. Whenever they stopped, a running debate took place about the size or shape of the barn in the photo and whether or not it matched the barn in front of them. So far they'd come up with a big, whopping zero. The women became more subdued with each structure that did not resemble the barn from the cross-stitch.

Finally, Annie said, "We should head back and try searching closer to Stony Point. The beach scene was close to Grey Gables, so the barn must be closer too."

"I think Annie is right." Alice backed up her friend's theory. "Betsy didn't travel much, especially after her husband passed on. I know we haven't determined when the cross-stitch was done, but it makes sense that she'd base all the scenes in or around Stony Point. There's such a … personal feeling to the piece. Maybe it was meant for someone at home."

"We'll just keep looking," Gwendolyn told them, undeterred as she folded the map to place back in her bag. "If Betsy meant for us to locate the scene, then we will."

Reluctantly, the others agreed. Mary Beth turned the SUV around, but insisted they stop for lunch before returning home. "We've come this far. We deserve a break."

Heading to the main route, they stopped at Lilia's Tea House—a quaint pink and purple cottage with gingerbread lattice. Once seated, the women regrouped and chatted about their day. Before long, and with the help of a sampling of flavored teas and sugary treats, they got their second wind and the energy to keep searching.

After lunch, the women stopped at a few yarn stores along the route before heading home. It was midafternoon by the time they crossed into Stony Point, passing a group of residential homes clustered together.

"Wait, wait, wait," Kate cried out. "Pull over."

On a dime, Mary Beth halted the vehicle. "What's wrong?"

"I told you I've had this nagging sense that I'd seen that barn."

"Around here?" Gwendolyn looked out the window. "I don't see anything."

"Mary Beth, drive around here for a minute," Kate instructed, her attention focused on her surroundings.

Mary Beth slowly accelerated and cruised the subdivision, coming to the end much too quickly.

"I could have sworn—" Kate mumbled in the back seat, still intently staring at the homes.

"I don't know about you," Peggy piped up. "But I'm ready to call it a day."

After a round of agreement from the women, Mary Beth headed toward Main Street. "We can always try another day."

"I think I can fit in another road trip," Gwendolyn assured them in a cheerful voice, hoping to raise their spirits.

They drove less than a minute when Kate called out, "This is it!"

Mary Beth squealed to a stop.

Kate opened the door and jumped out to face a two-story colonial home.

"That doesn't look like a barn," Peggy stated the obvious as she stepped from the SUV, eyes squinted as she viewed the house.

"It's not, Peggy." Kate ushered them down the driveway. "I know the family who lives here. I've dropped Vanessa off here many times, you know, for sleepovers or pool parties. I recall seeing a converted barn out back."

"Are you sure about this?" Peggy questioned, her brows

furrowed as she stood her ground.

"More than sure. Let's check it out. What have we got to lose?"

"How about getting arrested for trespassing," Alice deadpanned.

"Don't worry. I know the family who lives here. I'll let them know what we're doing."

The pace picked up as they followed Kate, anticipation spurring them on as they turned the corner and hurried into the backyard.

"Is that what I think it is?" Peggy squealed.

"I think so," Kate replied. As one, they all hurried to a barn nestled between tall pine trees, stopping before the structure, painted to match the white house with black trim.

"Okay, this could be it," Alice allowed. "It's in closer proximity to Grey Gables."

Mary Beth held out her hand to Annie. "Let's see the photo."

Annie removed it from her purse. Huddled together to check it, they darted glances between the picture and the actual barn. In the cross-stitch, Betsy had used a different color scheme than that of the building before them, but there was a definite correlation in the shadowing of pine trees. The markings stitched on Betsy's barn could also be used to compare the two.

"Anything match?" Mary Beth asked as she stepped closer to the structure.

Annie studied the image in the photo. "There's a weather vane on the roof in the cross-stitch."

Peggy looked up. "Not now. It must have been

removed since Betsy stitched the scene."

"It has a gambrel roof," Mary Beth pointed out. "Like it's an old-fashioned wood structure, not like those new steel barns folks use now."

"If it was painted red with white trim, it would be a perfect match," Peggy grumbled. "Which it's not."

Annie continued to view the photo. "Okay, there's a shovel leaning against the wall, but that won't help."

"Wait," Kate cried. "Look at the door leading to the hayloft."

Heads went back, and everyone gazed up over the large access door to the smaller, window-sized door.

"In the cross-stitch, isn't there a design in the wood door?" Kate asked.

Annie compared the photo and the hayloft door. "You're right. The strips of wood are crisscrossed twice with a smaller cross pattern at the apex of each one." She tried to contain her excitement, but failed. "My grandmother didn't make up the design. She used this as her model."

Mary Beth opened her mouth, dumbfounded. After a second, she found her voice. "We did it. We uncovered a clue."

Annie hugged a beaming Kate.

"I can't believe we found the barn because of me," Kate said with surprise.

"Hey, I'm glad you went with your gut. I never would have thought to look here."

"Neither did we." Alice playfully patted Kate on the back. "Of course, we could always thank Vanessa."

"Oh, don't you worry. I will, for all of us, as soon as I get home."

Annie dug around in her purse for the digital camera. "I've got to take a picture for LeeAnn." She leveled a telling gaze at Alice. "To prove I'm not obsessed."

She took a few shots of the barn, then had the women gathered together in front of the large door. "Proof positive we make a great team."

About this time a woman walked out the back door, a questioning smile on her lips as she approached Kate.

"Now would be a good time to explain," Kate said, hurrying away from the group to speak to the homeowner.

Holding up three fingers, Peggy said, "Three down, one to go," as they trooped back to the SUV. "We're on a roll."

A self-satisfied grin curved Gwendolyn's lips. "John thought this was a wild goose chase. He went golfing with his buddies this afternoon. I can't wait to tell him we found the barn. That should quiet him down."

"Men," Peggy scoffed in the spirit of sisterhood.

Gwendolyn's eyes sparkled as they all climbed back into the SUV to head home. "Seems I'm the one who scored today. And knowing my husband's golf swing, he couldn't hit the broad side of a barn."

~ 13 ~

Rain kept Annie cooped up in the house for the next week, which meant no more road trips to find the last clue until the weather cleared up. She took the opportunity to start removing all the old wallpaper in the kitchen to ready the walls for painting. The job took more time and effort than she originally thought. Some of the paper had been on the walls for years, hiding multiple layers, especially the borders, which were high and hard to reach. Annie hadn't used this much elbow grease in years, but she did now, scraping until her muscles ached. When she finally got down to the plaster, she breathed in relief, thankful the hard part was over.

She'd just climbed down the ladder when the doorbell rang. Hoping it was Alice so she had an excuse to take a break, Annie answered the door, only to find a stranger standing on the doorstep. Alarm skittered over her.

"Mrs. Dawson?"

"Yes."

"I'm Roger Smith." The man, in his thirties, handed her a business card. "If you aren't busy, I'd like to talk to you about the Betsy Original. May I come in?"

Speechless for a moment, Annie took the card that did indeed have his name and a telephone number on it, along with the title, Collector. Nothing else. She looked back at him, at the pleasant smile, the expensive suit. But his eyes sent a shiver down her spine. Dark and dangerous were the words that came to mind. She gripped the door handle more tightly, afraid to do more than breathe as normally as possible and keep her voice even as she spoke.

"What about it?"

When she didn't invite this stranger in, his eyes narrowed for a fraction of a second before he continued in a less than jovial voice. "I wanted to discuss purchasing the piece."

"It's not for sale."

"Everything has a price, Mrs. Dawson."

"Not this piece."

"Let me tell you what I'd like to offer—"

"There's really nothing to discuss, Mr. Smith. You've wasted your time coming here today."

He hesitated a moment. "Why don't you think about it, then give me a call?"

"There's nothing to think about. It's not for sale."

Realizing she wasn't going to budge, the man nodded, forcing a smile. "Just keep me in mind. Good afternoon."

With that, he turned and walked to his car. She watched him until he disappeared from view. How on earth had a collector found out about the Betsy Original?

Of course, thought Annie, it was Mary Beth. She'd been so excited about the Original that she was talking to her customers about it. She should have realized this would happen once word got out that a newly discovered Betsy Original had surfaced.

But this man ... she couldn't quite pinpoint the uncomfortable sensation that washed over her as he spoke.

He wasn't like any needlecraft collector she'd ever seen. Finally, she closed the door, her feet dragging as she walked into the living room.

She gazed at the Lady in the Attic, mentally asking questions she had no answers to. Compared to a few weeks ago when she had first found the cross-stitch, she could now identify three of the four scenes. She'd added every bit of information to her clue list, but it still didn't give any hints as to the identity of the woman. Mix in the strange events and now this stranger wanting to buy the piece, and her trouble radar went into high alert.

Annie still couldn't determine why her grandmother had picked this particular woman to be so prominent in the piece. And since Betsy hadn't left any written info, other than the letter that may or may not have been written by her, it still didn't help their discovery. Annie was no closer to finding the identity of the Lady than the day she found the framed piece in the attic, a fact that was really starting to bother her.

And now a stranger wanted to buy the Original. Annie would never sell it, of that she was sure. There was no amount of money that would make her part with her grandmother's work. And she had a feeling that this guy showing up might be the first of others who would want to purchase the piece. She sighed. Things never got easier, did they?

The work on the house kept Annie busy, and the week blended into the next. She even missed the next Hook and Needle Club meeting. When she called Mary Beth to let her know she was still tied up at the house, Mary Beth expressed her disappointment, as the women were still pretty high on the victory of finding a clue to the cross-stitch. But she also understood that Annie needed to get this remodeling job done, that her focus needed to be on Grey Gables for a while.

In the midsummer, thunderclouds could linger for days. And as the overcast weather continued, Annie took out her frustration over not being able to hunt for clues by painting and sanding the floors, pretty much anything that would move the work load along.

By the following Friday, the sun finally broke through the gloom, ushering in the month of August. After being cooped up all week, Annie ventured out to the grocery store. Dressed in her work clothes of old jeans, oversized T-shirt, and sneakers, she hit the store for a few much-needed items, coffee being at the top of the list. Her stash was seriously low; if she wanted to make it through the up-coming days of painting, she needed a fresh supply. It was early enough to get in and out of the store without anyone catching her dressed this way. At least that was the plan, until she literally ran straight into Stella. Or at least her shopping cart did.

"Stella. I'm sorry, I wasn't paying attention."

"I can see that. No doubt daydreaming about your mystery."

Annie smiled despite the woman's sour expression at the sight of Annie's clothes. Annie knew she looked pretty ratty today, so she couldn't blame Stella for her reaction. "Actually, I was thinking about all I have to do at Grey Gables."

"So you've put the house on the market?"

"No."

"Then why bother with all the work?"

So much for subtlety. "Because I like living there. I enjoy fixing it up."

Stella merely humphed.

Clenching her teeth, Annie decided to change the subject. Stella wasn't going to change her views on the current ownership of Grey Gables, and Annie wasn't going to try to persuade her otherwise. "I missed the Hook and Needle Club meeting this week. Were you able to make it?"

"No. I've had to put my knitting aside just now." A slight frown marred Stella's forehead. "Although I do hear from one of the girls daily."

"We all agree that it's not the same without you there."

"And now you've become part of 'we all'?"

Annie's heart sank. She thought she'd been making strides fitting in here. Could she be mistaken? Had she taken her accepted presence in town for granted? She wasn't sure she wanted the answers to those questions.

To cover her disquiet, she said instead, "I'd like to think so. You've all been kind to include me in your club. And I'm excited about the new project ideas."

Stella's high and lofty expression softened and grew a bit secretive. "I've been busy with a few projects of my own."

Hmm. The rumors were true then. Stella did have something going on. As long as Stella seemed inclined to hint about it, Annie would take the bait. "What would that be?"

She shrugged. "I'm not at liberty to discuss anything at this point."

Judging by the expectant look on Stella's face, clearly she wanted to, so Annie prodded. "You have your own mystery going on?"

Stella puffed up. "Yes, you could say that I do."

Finally, she'd made points. "Well, good for you. When you're ready, I'd love to hear all about it."

"Why?"

"Why would I be interested?"

"Yes."

"I've heard the others talk about your involvement on museum boards and how you were involved with art projects in New York. I have to imagine you've got some great plans in store for Stony Point."

The flattery made Stella's lips curl up at the corners, which could almost be construed as a smile. "I'm still in the planning stages."

"That's why I can't wait to hear about it, whatever you have planned."

Stella's eyes narrowed as she regarded Annie suspiciously. "You'll hear about it with the others."

"That means we'll see you Tuesday?"

"If I can make it."

The silence grew awkward after that, but Stella didn't leave. Annie stood there for another moment longer, unsure where to go. As she was trying to decide how to handle the situation, Stella's Jason approached. A tall man with thick black hair shot through with strands of gray, his tanned face lined by years of smiles, he appeared to be in his sixties, but his obvious good health made it hard to pinpoint. Dressed in a striped polo shirt, tan Dockers, and outrageously red sneakers, he looked like a man ready to hit the golf course, not chauffeur Stella around town.

"The Lincoln's out front, ready when you are," he said with a jovial tone, heavily laced in New Yorkese. He spied Annie and stuck out his hand. "Hello. I'm Jason."

Annie retuned the greeting. "Annie Dawson."

His eyes twinkled. "The other outsider?"

"Yes. From Texas."

"Brooklyn, born and raised."

"That would explain the accent."

"I was gonna say the same thing."

"Do you miss the hustle of the big city?"

"At first. Couldn't get used to all this quiet. Those crickets sure bugged me when I first arrived."

"And now?"

"Now I'm used to it. Mrs. Brickson keeps me busy, but she lets me get home a couple times a year." He grinned, not one bit concerned about Stella's evil eye. "She says sending me back to my roots makes me appreciate my job more."

"Does that work?"

"Yep. Every time I have to fight city traffic or listen to sirens 24-7, I'm thankful I now live in a place that's peaceful." He took a step closer and lowered his voice. "She even has me working in her yard. Never did that back home."

"It is soothing."

"Not when Mrs. Brickson is issuing orders."

"I heard that, Jason."

Even though Stella wore a scowl, Annie could see she had a soft spot for the man. She suspected Stella depended on him more than she'd ever admit.

Stella angled her cart toward the front of the store. "We should be going."

"Right." Jason winked at Annie. "Secret meetings and all that."

Stella snorted. "They aren't secret if you announce it to the world."

"Mrs. Brickson, you keep forgetting that this is a small town. Can't keep much secret around here."

"I can try," she muttered as she passed Annie.

"Nice meeting you," Annie told him.

"I'm sure we'll bump into each other again."

Annie watched Stella's retreat, wishing she could patch up the problem between them. She had no idea where to start. Guess she'd just have to cover Stella with kindness and hope the woman changed her outlook.

*   *   *   *

After days of dressing for a mess, Annie decided to go "girly," wearing a cotton sundress in a soft shade of coral and low white sandals. She arrived early the following Tuesday for the Hook and Needle Club meeting, and for the first time since she'd been invited, she got there before the other ladies.

Mary Beth greeted her warmly, setting aside her disappointment in Annie for missing a meeting. "We missed you last week."

"And I missed ya'll too, but you wouldn't believe the work I've accomplished. The grand old house is really starting to shape up."

"We've heard. Wally told Peggy the work is coming along."

"Wally is a great handyman. Alone, I couldn't have done a fraction of the work he's done. I really appreciate his help."

"Not any more than they appreciate the work. Usually he gets more jobs during the summer when folks come to evaluate the condition of their summer homes and see firsthand the work needed after a hard winter. I'm assuming Grey Gables is more than just one winter's worth of work."

"You'd think, but the house has really held up over the years. The exterior needed most of the attention, and Wally's finished the difficult part. He mentioned taking another job, so the timing worked for both of us." Annie placed her tote on one of the chairs in the circle. "The inside is mostly cosmetic. The painting seems endless, but in the long run, the transformation will be amazing."

Mary Beth joined her, a knowing grin on her lips. "Since you've been busy, does that mean you haven't been crocheting?"

"To be honest, not really."

"Then you need to catch up."

"The blanket is nearly finished. It's the fall project I'm stumped about. That's why I came by early today. I wanted to ask what you think I should do."

To Annie, this new project wasn't about coming up with the most clever or unusual crocheted item. No, this project was more about Annie making inroads to the community. Hoping to be accepted as one of the Hook and Needle Club members, not Betsy's visiting granddaughter.

"That's part of the fun of this group project. Everyone comes up with her own idea."

"I've been so busy with the house, I haven't had a chance

to really sit down and explore the possibilities."

"I've noticed you admiring Kate's work. Why not ask her for pointers? I know she'd appreciate it."

"I think I'll do that. If you don't mind," Annie said, "I'm going to look over your book rack and see if any ideas catch my eye."

"You know," Mary Beth said from across the room, "I've been thinking a lot about your Betsy Original."

"Now that you mention it, I wanted to ask you something. Have you had any collectors asking about the piece?"

Mary Beth frowned. "No. I've mentioned it to some customers and someone from the New England Stitch Club, but not in the context of it being for sale. Why do you ask?"

"I've had an offer."

"Really?" Mary Beth's hand flew to her throat. "I hope I haven't started a problem."

Somehow, Annie couldn't see Mary Beth doing business with the man who'd shown up on her porch. "No. I just wanted to know if I could expect more offers."

"Honestly, I don't know."

Annie shrugged, hiding her doubts. She didn't want Mary Beth to worry about this.

"Well, as I was saying, I always got the feeling your grandmother never did anything randomly. Have you thought any more about why she created it?"

"Believe me, I've wracked my brain over just that. Trouble is, nothing specific stands out to me." Annie hesitated. Much as she tried, she couldn't think of any conversation she'd had with her grandmother that would relate to it. Betsy had simply never alluded to it at all. Yet she'd taken great care to protect the piece while it was stored in the attic. And that was the kicker. Betsy never kept her work up there. Even as she worked on a design, she kept her fabric and floss handy in a basket by her favorite chair so she could stitch whenever time allowed. What had caused her to hide this particular piece?

"Then it must have been special to her, don't you think?"

"All her pieces were special, but this one seems to stand out. It's so elaborate. That's why I don't understand why she kept it in the attic." Annie removed a crochet book that interested her and wandered back to the circle. "If my grandmother left any clues she intended for me to find, she hid them well, because I haven't found anything to go on."

"I just have a hard time seeing Betsy as ... a schemer. She was always straightforward."

"Trust me, she could be wily at times. Especially when she wanted me to do a chore or two without making it look like work."

"I think that's a trait all grandmothers possess."

"She even roped Alice in a few times."

"And I bet you both had a ball. Why I remember—"

Just then the door burst open and Peggy ran inside, her face flushed and her eyes wide.

"You aren't going to believe this. I just heard from Matty Waters, who was talking to Sue Lancaster, who knows Edie Borman. Edie is a member of the Historical Society but also part of Stella's other group of friends." She stopped to catch a much-needed breath. "And do you know what Edie supposedly said?"

Mary Beth grinned. "I can't imagine."

"Stella and Liz have formed a committee to start a new cultural center, and she wants the first exhibit to be about textiles. She wants to have a fund-raiser to promote the exhibit."

"Gee," Alice drawled as she and Kate strolled in during Peggy's tirade. "Wonder where she got that idea from?"

"From Mary Beth."

"Sometimes Peggy misses sarcasm," Alice whispered to Annie.

"That will interfere with our project. What are we going to do?" Peggy demanded.

"I don't think there's much we can do." Mary Beth patted Peggy's arm and led her to a chair. "Once Stella makes up her mind, she's pretty hard to stop."

Peggy sank into a chair. "It's not right. She stole our idea."

"Mary Beth's idea," Alice corrected.

"What about Mary Beth's idea?" Gwendolyn asked as she breezed through the door.

Peggy jumped up and relayed the story again.

"Oh my. She isn't terribly original."

Peggy crossed her arms over her chest, a mutinous frown on her face. "She should have asked us to be a part of this."

"Ah, the crux of the problem." Mary Beth joined the younger woman, placing an arm around her shoulders. A sense of hurt laced Mary Beth's voice. "You're right, though. She could have asked us to participate."

Gwendolyn unpacked her yarn and needles. "We would have been the logical people to ask."

Annie intently watched the women's downcast faces. Anger started to roil in the pit of her stomach. Stella may not like the idea of the club's interest in a new Betsy Original, but that was no reason to hurt her friends. And worse, they'd been loyal, staying in touch even though Stella had left the group. If she was only doing this to get back at Annie for breaking the status quo by being welcomed into the club, would the women rally around Annie as they had Stella? After all, Annie was the newest member. Stella had made it more than clear that she'd like Annie to go back to Texas. Would they all agree? No matter how Annie analyzed it, it all came back to Stella acting out once Annie arrived.

"Is there any way to change her mind?" Alice asked.

"Sure," Annie shrugged. "Stop looking for clues about the Lady in the Attic."

Peggy's face scrunched in confusion. "Who?"

Annie grinned sheepishly. "That's what I named the woman in the cross-stitch."

"Cute," Alice said, "but I doubt we want to stop looking now. We've come so far."

Gwendolyn studied the piece she'd been knitting. "This's true."

"I agree," Mary Beth added.

"And we don't want to call Stella out on this?" Alice continued.

"Well, maybe you should ..." Annie started.

"But she is our friend," Mary Beth finished. "At least I thought she was."

Silence filled the room as the ladies contemplated their newest dilemma.

"There's two ways to handle this," Gwendolyn finally announced. "We ignore the fact that Stella wants to do a fund-raiser without us, or we confront Stella and let her know she's hurt our feelings by not including us.

"In the years we've known Stella, we've seen her try to get the cultural center started more than once, but something always keeps her plans from moving forward. Maybe she's afraid things will fall apart again before the final stages, and she'll be embarrassed. If we act like her plans don't bother us, and this time she's successful in opening the center, then she may very well include us later on."

"I'd forgotten about that," Kate, who had been silent this whole time, spoke softly as she sat in the chair next to Peggy. "Maybe she hasn't even considered that her new plans would bother us."

"Well, this does bother us," Peggy pouted.

"We can't let her see that," Kate replied. "Remember how we all agreed to keep tabs on Stella while she stays away from the club meetings? Now would be an easy time to stop calling her. And knowing Stella, she'll need our friendship if nothing comes from her plans for the center."

Mary Beth rose up to her whole five foot, two inches. "If I may be the spokeswoman of the club?"

As if she wasn't already.

"Gwendolyn and Kate are right. We ought to go on with life as normal. Don't encourage Stella, but don't let on like this affects us one little bit. We wait and see if this cultural center really happens. Between all of us, we have plenty of pieces to add to a textile exhibit if she asks. We'll wait her out. She may be using the cultural center as an excuse to stay away from our mystery, but we can't jump to conclusions, just in case the center opens. And we do want Stella to succeed, don't we?"

"And if she still doesn't include us in the fund-raiser?" Annie asked.

"Then we have an ace in the hole. The Lady in the Attic."

Alice grinned at Mary Beth. "I like the way you think."

"It's a gift."

The others laughed, but Annie couldn't control the unease swirling in her stomach. If anyone had the perfect item to add to a textile exhibit, the clincher and drawing piece would be Betsy's newly found Original. Annie grew sick at the thought. She didn't want her grandmother's work used as a pawn. She may not know why her grandmother had created the Lady, but she was sure Betsy never had this in mind.

Even though the ladies thought the Lady was an ace in the hole, Annie decided not to mention the fact that she hadn't agreed to display it anywhere, let alone at a new cultural center. Nor that she'd had a strange offer from a buyer. There was still an emotional bond to the piece that she couldn't ignore, and because of that, she refused to even think about its future.

She glanced around the room as the women, her friends, discussed the latest drama. Stella may think she was making a point with her little mutiny, but, if anything, her actions brought the club members closer together by solving this mystery. What had started out as a solo effort for Annie had turned into a team endeavor.

Which made Annie more determined to uncover the secrets behind the Lady in the Attic.

～ 14 ～

After the Hook and Needle Club meeting, Annie stopped by The Cup & Saucer for a quick lunch. She'd taken a seat and placed her order when the door opened, and Mr. Smith walked in. He gazed around the room, his eyes lighting up when he glimpsed her. Determination written on his face, he quickly crossed the room.

"Do you mind if I join you?"

"Actually, I do. I'm waiting for someone." She hated to fib, really she did, but there was no way she was going to have a prolonged conversation with this man. Once again, he'd set off all her warning bells.

"Then I'll get to the point. I'm still interested in purchasing the Betsy Original. I can definitely make it worth your while."

"My decision hasn't changed. I am not selling the piece."

"Look, if you'd just let me ..."

The door opened and Ian walked in. Annie raised her hand to wave him over. "Here I am," she called out loudly.

Puzzled but pleased, Ian headed in her direction.

"I'm so glad you could make it," she said to Ian, then glanced back at Mr. Smith. "I think we're finished," she told him.

Mr. Smith took a quick look at Ian and nodded.

As he exited the restaurant, Annie released a puff of

breath and looked up at Ian. "Sorry about that."

"Care to explain?" he asked, taking a seat across the table.

"Mr. Smith wants to buy the Betsy Original."

"Let me guess. It's not for sale."

She nodded. "He has a hard time accepting the word 'no.'"

Ian raised a questioning eyebrow.

Annie proceeded to tell him about Mr. Smith's first visit and the strange happenings at Grey Gables.

His frown grew deeper as she spoke. "I have to say, I'm not sure I like any of this."

"Me neither. Eventually he'll get the message."

"Are you okay?"

"Yes. I've been locking my doors and looking over my shoulder."

"You have my number. Give me a call if this guy bothers you again. Or if you notice anything out of the ordinary at Grey Gables."

"Thanks. Boots and I will be fine."

He grinned. "Why doesn't that surprise me?"

The waitress stopped by for Ian's order and as they ate lunch, Annie changed the subject. Mr. Smith's offer still loomed in the back of her mind, but she felt better finally telling someone about her concerns.

On the way home, she called Alice and asked her to stop by that afternoon. With all the talk at the meeting about Stella and the Lady in the Attic, Annie realized they needed to step up efforts to find the last clue. Since no one recognized the house scene stitched on the cloth, she thought maybe she'd find answers by finally organizing Gram's room. A tall order, since Gram had stored years of stuff in her room.

Annie knew this would be a consuming undertaking, and she'd been putting it off, not wanting to disturb her grandmother's personal belongings until necessary. Now it seemed that the time had finally come to clean out the bedroom.

Not looking forward to tackling the task alone, she was glad Alice was free this afternoon. Really, Alice was the one person Annie felt comfortable with helping sort out Gram's things, since she'd spent as much time at Grey Gables as Annie. Intently vague, Annie had dangled the bait about desperately needing Alice's help. Even though she didn't know what the job entailed, Alice had readily volunteered.

"What's so important you lured me over here?" Alice asked as soon as she stepped into Grey Gables.

"I thought it was time to tidy Gram's bedroom. There must be clues from Gram around here somewhere, but her room seems the most logical. She kept her most personal possessions there. Problem is, I really couldn't bear straightening up her room alone."

Alice patted Annie's arm. "I understand. And I'm glad to help."

Annie expelled a heavy breath filled with gratitude. "Thanks."

"Okay, where do we start?" 'Take-Charge Alice' asked as she pushed up her sleeves, a willing participant in Annie's plan.

"Wait here."

She left Alice in the kitchen and hurried to the library, collecting the letter she'd found in the attic with the frame.

"Before we start anywhere, tell me what you think of this."

As Annie handed the letter to Alice, her brow knitted as she took it. "You were holding out on me?"

"Actually, I didn't think this letter would help us, but take a look anyway. I found it the first day, tucked in the back of the frame. I read it that night, then set it aside.

"At first I thought it just got wedged between the cloth and wood, but it must have a purpose. I went back to the attic to see if there was anything else in the general area that might be useful, but didn't find anything."

Alice read out loud, her perplexed reaction matching Annie's when she first read it. *"To the Sister of my heart, this is for you."* She glanced at Annie. "Betsy wrote this?"

"I don't know. The handwriting isn't exactly like Gram's, at least in her later years, but that doesn't mean she couldn't have written it back when her handwriting was steady."

Alice studied it more closely. "She did give me a list of groceries from time to time, but I don't recall enough to say it matches."

"For now, we can add this as another clue."

"Except we don't know to whom she wrote it or why. Its meaning is beautiful but very vague."

"That's why we need to find out who the Lady is. Or was. It will solve every question we have."

"What's your game plan?"

"We tidy up Gram's bedroom. If she left any personal clues, that would be the room."

"I thought you scoured the entire house for clues when you were cleaning and painting."

"I did, but I couldn't bring myself to rifle through Gram's things." As long as her grandmother's belongings went untouched, Annie felt the comforting presence of the older woman. Lasting memories she could hold onto as long as she lived in the house.

Now, in the light of Stella's latest move, the fate of the cross-stitch not only affected Annie and her future once they determined the identity of the young woman, but it also intertwined the members of the Hook and Needle Club, who had become almost as invested in the outcome as Annie herself.

"We have our work cut out for us."

"You have no idea." Annie cast a mischievous smile Alice's way.

"I did make up the bed after Betsy died, but otherwise, I haven't been up there since we were kids."

Annie swept her arms in the direction of the second floor. "Follow me."

"This seems strange," Alice said as they entered the room. "I feel like I'm twelve years old again."

"Yeah, that was my first thought. I've settled my clothes in my old room, but I've slept here since I arrived. I find it comforting."

Alice took a few tentative steps deeper into the room. "It smells like Betsy. What was that perfume she always wore?"

"Emeraude. She never left home without spritzing herself with it." Annie crossed to the dresser, lifting a perfume bottle as she gazed around the room.

The old four-poster bed topped with homemade quilts beckoned Annie to rest her head at night. A wide dresser with an attached mirror held scattered bottles, boxes, and jewelry on top, overstuffed drawers below. In the corner of the room, a rocking chair faced the window, drawing weary souls to sit and gaze out over the property, the ocean in the distance. On the surface of a French-style writing desk, papers collected in untidy piles. Nearby, books spilled from an overloaded bookshelf. All an integral part of Betsy Holden's life.

Enough woolgathering, she thought to herself. Annie set down the bottle and crossed to the closet. "Ready?"

Alice nodded and Annie pulled open the door, a little afraid the movement might cause items to tumble out all around them. Thankfully, everything stayed precariously inside.

"What was Betsy thinking?" Alice asked as she stood at the threshold. "How did she cram so much stuff in here?"

"Good question. Believe me, I've asked myself the same thing. Apparently, Gram was the definition of a pack rat. You think this is bad? You should see the attic."

"How on earth does one person collect all this?"

"If you figure she lived here for well over fifty years, that's a lot of time to fill up space."

"Here's a horrible thought. What if she ran out of storage space here *and* in the attic, and then stored stuff elsewhere? Have you been to the basement?"

Annie shuddered. "Once, and I have to say, it's my least favorite place in the entire house. It's damp and dark and better left to someone who isn't creeped out by crawly things."

"Good. I don't like basements either. Spiders and shadowy corners are not my cup of tea."

"Me neither. Let's make a pact. Even if we don't find any clues up here, the basement is off limits. I've seen enough movies to know nothing good ever comes from going down there."

"I agree wholeheartedly."

Annie held her index and middle fingers out toward Alice, just like they used to do as kids. "Pact?"

Alice giggled and held up her same fingers and pressed them against Annie's. "Pact."

"Let's get started." Annie nodded toward the dresser. "Since you're the guest, you can start there. I'll take the closet."

"And we're looking for what, exactly?"

"Anything that looks like a clue. Maybe another cross-stitch project. A letter hidden in a box. A picture. Who knows?"

"Sheesh. How about a neon sign with an arrow that says 'woman's identity hidden here.' "

"That would be great."

"Yeah, well, don't hold your breath." Alice opened a drawer and rifled inside. "There's always the possibility the woman in the piece is just your grandmother's imagination."

"I can't go there. This has become too personal to me. Besides, why else go from the usual style that she was famous for and try a completely different style unless it meant something?"

"And what if she started the piece years ago and decided she didn't like stitching people?"

Annie tugged at a trunk, pulling it into the room to pry open the top. "I checked the stitching of the woman against one of her earlier works. The type of stitching she did for the Lady in the Attic resembles her most current work. I know everyone thinks you just make x's on the cloth, but Gram would outline the work in certain colors that were unusual and gave the scene flair, like a 3-D look. Or she'd add some embroidery stitches for substance. I'm not sure how she decided when to use different stitches, I just know that's what made her work *original*."

"That makes sense." Alice stopped and pulled a crocheted shawl from deep within a drawer. "Annie, look at this. How beautiful."

And it was, made of fine sea-green yarn with metallic strands running through it; it shimmered in the afternoon sun streaming through the window. The delicate stitches, formed in a pattern in multiples of two, made the shawl as stunning as it was functional.

"I remember my grandmother working on that one summer when I was here." Taking it from Alice, Annie held the soft piece open to inspect it better. She remembered Gram saying the green reminded her of the ocean in springtime. The design and stitching, so vintage, yet understated, added to the classic inventory of another lovely Betsy creation. She folded it and handed it back to Alice. "Why don't you keep it?"

"What? No way."

"I think it will look lovely on you."

Alice's eyes grew bright, her voice wobbly. "I don't know what to say."

"Say, 'Thank you, Annie,' and take it home and enjoy it."

"Thanks, Annie. Really."

"You're welcome. Really."

The next two hours flew by as Annie tore through boxes from the closet and Alice dug through dresser drawers while walking down memory lane. They recalled the summers they'd spent up here, camped out in Gram's bedroom—even though Annie's room would have been big enough—playing dress-up with old clothes found in a worn-out chest. Or the teen years when they shared secret crushes, makeup tips, and dreams about the future. As they reminisced, Annie pulled two broad-brimmed straw hats from the far back top shelf.

"Remember when we wore these to have high tea with our dolls?" Annie ran her fingers over a frayed brim lined with a faded pink ribbon. "I don't remember them being so ratty looking."

"I'm sure we didn't notice. Then again, that was a few decades ago."

"Don't remind me."

Alice pulled an old cigar box from deep in the bottom drawer. "Hey, look at this." She moved to sit on the edge of the bed. Annie joined her. Boots, having deemed herself worthy to grace them with her presence as they worked, jumped up on the bed and circled around before dropping onto the quilted coverlet for a nap.

Alice opened the box. Inside, nestled in a bed of cotton material, lay two dog-eared movie tickets, a candy wrapper, an aged, yellowed hankie with blue flowers stitched into one corner, and a silver frame.

The photo in the frame, an old black and white, featured two young women, their backs to the camera, arms slung across each other's shoulders.

"This is definitely Gram," she said, pointing to the girl on the right. "She always had her hair pinned up like that in the back, but her hair was heavy and constantly slipped out, with wisps trailing down her back."

Alice looked closely. "The other girl has her hair pinned up in the same way, but not a strand out of place."

"And look at the clothes. Even in black and white, you can tell that Gram's dress is worn while the other girl's seems more fashionable and in better shape. But I don't know who it is." Annie sighed with frustration. "What do you say we take a break and bring the photo downstairs to get a better look?"

"Sounds good. I could use something to drink."

Once downstairs, Annie placed the frame on the table. "Coffee or iced tea?"

"Iced tea would be great." Alice wiped the sheen from her brow. The afternoon heat had definitely crept in.

Annie filled two glasses and delivered them to the table. She crossed the room to retrieve a magnifying glass from a kitchen drawer before sitting down. She handed the magnifier to Alice, who had slipped the thumb-worn photo from the picture frame.

"Nothing written on the back." She turned it over and peered closely. "They must have been down at the docks. I can make out part of a boat here."

"I noticed that," Annie said, barely containing the eagerness in her voice. She pointed to the background. "I think my great-grandfather worked on a boat. Lobster probably, but I don't remember."

Alice continued to examine the picture. "Uh, Annie? Is it my imagination or do the clothes on the other woman resemble the ones worn in the cross-stitch?"

Annie took the picture from Alice's fingers. The first tingles of excitement surged through her as she came to the same conclusion. "They look similar."

"Could that be our mystery lady?"

"I don't know. But this is the closest we've come to finding anything that resembles her."

Annie carefully placed the photo back in the frame, hopeful for the first time since they'd found the previous clue.

After a few long moments, Alice tapped her hand on the table. "Okay, with all the clutter in your grandmother's room, we definitely found something useful."

"True, but we still don't know who the woman is."

"This is not the time to get discouraged," said Alice, newly energized.

"I'm not discouraged. More frustrated than anything else. Now we have two mystery women!"

"C'mon Annie, you have to be positive. I think she and the Lady in the Attic are one and the same. We have to go with that."

Annie glanced at her vivacious friend and said dryly, "That's right. You were a cheerleader in high school."

"And a darned good one." Alice's smile shined one hundred watts. "Now what?"

Annie stared at the photo. "Maybe Gwendolyn would have an idea who it is if we showed her." She glanced at her watch. "Think it's too close to dinner to call her?"

Alice jumped up to grab the telephone receiver. "It never hurts to try. If she's home, we could walk over."

Ten minutes later they were knocking on Gwendolyn's back door. She came out and ushered them to a shaded patio table with glasses of tea all ready for them. Annie handed her the photo, along with the letter she decided to bring along at the last minute.

"I found these at Gram's. The letter was with the Betsy

Original, and the picture frame was hidden in a dresser drawer."

"This is exciting!" Gwendolyn motioned them to sit as Annie handed her the magnifying glass as well. She studied both very carefully for what felt like an eternity to Annie.

"The letter is intriguing," Gwendolyn finally said, "but unfortunately I'm not familiar enough with Betsy's handwriting to tell if it's hers. Her stitches? Now those were her trademark. I could distinguish them immediately." She held the photo closer. "I agree that this is probably your grandmother in the picture, but I'm sorry to say I don't know who the other woman is." She looked up, the twinkle in her eyes matching the full smile on her lips. "But the clothing matches the cross-stitch. Is she our mystery woman?"

"That's what we thought."

"Hmm."

A commotion sounded in the kitchen, followed by John joining them on the patio. "Good evening, ladies. What are you up to?"

"Do you recognize anything in this picture?" Gwendolyn asked as she handed him the snapshot.

He pulled on his glasses and studied the photo with serious concentration. "I believe this was a lobster boat that was part of a fleet." He removed his glasses and pointed to the boat. "Years ago a lot of independent fishermen used the docks as their base of operations. But there were also companies that owned two or three vessels. Most of the men in town worked on the boats or at the docks. Like my uncle."

Hope flared through Annie. "Maybe he could give us some insight."

John shook his head. "He passed away many years ago."

"Maybe we could find out who owned the boats," Alice suggested. "Narrow it down from there."

"I don't know where you'd begin to find information like that. Perhaps old town records? Maybe the Historical Society?"

"We can't ask the Historical Society. Those are Stella's people," Alice remarked.

"We could ask Ian. He was helpful before."

"How will the boat help you find out who the people in the picture are?" John asked. "These women could have been down on the docks one day to visit and someone took a random shot. That boat might not mean anything in your search."

"Back to square one," Alice muttered.

"Not really," Gwendolyn corrected her.

"How's that?"

"All along we've questioned whether your grandmother based the woman in the cross-stitch after a real person or if she simply used her vivid imagination." She nodded to the photo in her husband's hand. "If the woman in the snapshot is indeed our mystery woman, then at the very least, I would say that this proves your Lady in the Attic was very real."

～ 15 ～

On Thursday evening, Alice headed home from an afternoon Princessa party but had to make one last stop before she called it a day. She loved working the parties, but sometimes all the talking and smiling made her weary. Her former husband had accused her of always being the life of the party. Like that was a bad thing. Apparently to him, it was. *Don't go there*, she reminded herself. That part of her life was over. She'd moved on and couldn't afford unpleasant memories to drag her down.

As she steered her convertible onto Old Harbor Road, she slowed down to search for Nancy Roberts's house. She'd been given the referral at her last party and booked a date, so she needed to drop off literature on the Princessa line and answer any questions the hostess might have. Alice had scribbled down the address in her all-important planner. Squinting to make out the numbers on mailboxes, she finally found her destination and pulled into the driveway of a house set back from the road.

She gathered up the special hot pink Princessa hostess bag filled with party books and order forms. As she walked around the car, she stopped to admire the neat brick sidewalk leading up to the porch where pale pink and white impatiens bloomed wildly along the steps. The white front door created a bold focal point against the cozy clapboard house painted in federal blue with white shutters.

A sense of memory engulfed her. Had she been here before? Maybe held a Princessa party? She must be tired. Her usually excellent memory was fuzzy right about now, and she couldn't recall if she'd been here, but that didn't mean anything. In the past few years, she'd been to enough addresses in Stony Point to rival the mailman.

The door opened and a young woman with a baby on her hip and a toddler at her feet stepped out. A twinge hit Alice's heart, but she buried the feeling and pasted her saleswoman smile on her face.

"Hi, Mrs. Roberts," she called out. "I'm Alice MacFarlane. I just wanted to drop off the materials for your Princessa party next week."

"Thanks," Nancy answered, taking the older boy by the hand as they met Alice on the pathway. The tow-headed boys, who closely resembled their mother, shyly watched Alice approach.

"I appreciate your stopping by," Nancy told her. "I'm new in town and haven't been out and about much yet."

"All part of my service," Alice smiled. Confirming the date and time, they chatted a few moments before Alice made her goodbyes. She hurried back to the car, glad to finally go home, but she stopped to watch the threesome disappear into the house.

Sighing, she took one last look, frowned for a second, then did a double take. And a triple take. *No way!* She'd been right—thinking this house seemed familiar to her. With her breath caught in her throat, she leaned inside the car to grab her purse and pull out her phone. Punching in the numbers she had memorized, she waited impatiently for an answer.

"Annie, I think I might have found the last scene from the Lady in the Attic," she blurted after her friend said hello.

"Alice?"

"Yes, it's Alice. Who else would call you in a panic about the Betsy Original?"

"Mary Beth, Peggy, Kate, or Gwendolyn?"

"Okay, you got me, but really, I think I have a lead."

"Where are you?"

"Just south of town on the Old Harbor Road." She gave Annie directions. "And bring the picture of the house scene. Along with your camera," she added as an afterthought. "Your daughter will want to see this."

"I'll see you in ten."

Not wanting to alarm her new hostess, Alice backed her car out of the driveway and parked across the street. Once she spied Annie's car come around the corner, she got out of her Mustang and waited for Annie to park behind her.

Beaming, Alice rested her hip against the fender, arms crossed over her chest, a canary-eating grin on her lips, still stunned that she'd found a clue.

"Okay, what's all the fuss?" Annie asked, her face flushed as she joined Alice.

Alice nodded at the house and watched Annie's face until Annie glanced back with surprise. Then she pulled the picture from her purse and compared it with the real thing.

"So?" Alice pushed away from the car, expectancy written on her face. "What do you think?"

"It does resemble ..."

"Do you know how many times I've driven by here

and never paid attention to that house?"

"What changed today?"

"I came by to drop off a hostess packet before going home. I had this feeling like maybe I'd been here before, so I kept staring at the house. The more I looked, the more something tickled the edges of my memory. After a few minutes, I realized it was the house featured in the cross-stitch."

"I'm impressed," Annie teased. "You're becoming a regular Sherlock Holmes."

"I know. I'm getting good at this sleuthing thing."

"Yeah, well, don't give up your day job just yet."

"Hey, it's my day job that led me to the last clue."

Alice realized she'd really missed the camaraderie of a good friend. Maybe holding herself back and not getting out there again after the divorce hadn't been such a good plan. But then, who knew what to do after a divorce?

Annie dragged her out of her gloomy thoughts when she asked, "Who lives here?"

"Nancy Roberts."

"A long-time resident? Any relatives we can link her to?"

"Nope. She's new in town."

Annie puffed out a breath. "Any idea who lived here before?"

"No, it's changed homeowners a few times—at least that I can remember. A long time ago, when I was a kid, I think it was vacant and kind of fell into disrepair. I remember my mom saying it was a shame because the house was so lovely."

"Do you think your mom would remember who originally owned the place?"

"I could ask. She moved to Florida about ten years ago, but honestly, her memory is shot. My sister took her in last year to keep an eye on her."

"Maybe Gwendolyn will know."

Alice rubbed her hands up and down her arms, overcome with a tingly sensation. Because she had found the next clue to the cross-stitch? "I just got the weirdest feeling."

"That's how I felt the day on the beach when we turned up with the first scene."

"Your grandmother keeps reaching out to us, doesn't she?"

Annie visibly shivered. "I'm sure that wasn't her intent, but yes, she does."

Betsy's friendship had meant a lot to Alice. She'd been there with a ready smile, words of wisdom, or a warm piece of her amazing blueberry pie, just when Alice needed it the most. And now, when she needed a peer the most, her old friend Annie was back, their bond renewed. Wouldn't it be like Betsy to plan it that way? Along with a mystery to keep the women occupied, just like the old days when she'd found activities to keep two curious girls busy.

Alice took one last long look at the house. A warm blanket of comfort enveloped her, happiness filled her heart. "That makes figuring out the story behind the cross-stitch even better."

*   *   *   *

"We found the last clue," Annie told her daughter later that night when LeeAnn called after dinner. She stood at the sink, gazing out over the backyard.

"Okay, backtrack and fill me in on all the details."

Just as she had since this whole mystery started, Annie kept LeeAnn informed about their progress in phone conversations and letters. Anxious to share the latest news, Annie couldn't wait to tell her about Alice's discovery.

"It's funny how you can pass a house or a landmark and, over time, never really pay attention. The club has had a ball figuring out the scenes."

"Like you haven't? You've laughed more in the last few weeks than you have since Dad died."

"That's true." As much as Annie missed Wayne, she had enjoyed herself these past weeks. That didn't make her a bad person, did it? This is just what she'd wanted, right?

Annie got back to the topic at hand. "Unfortunately, finding the clue doesn't help. At least not yet, anyway. No one knows how it ties to your great-grandmother."

"Couldn't she have made things easier on you?"

"She could have, but it wouldn't have been as worthwhile."

"I suppose she had her reasons."

"Gram always did."

Her grandmother had given her a challenge. Not just the cross-stitch, but fitting into life here in Stony Point. And, as the summer progressed, Annie grew more confident in that particular challenge. And more intrigued by her grandmother's secrets.

They chatted about the grandchildren before LeeAnn returned to the original topic. "You know those letters you've sent me, kind of chronicling what's been going on in Stony Point? I'm going to keep them all together in a special stationery box. I think the kids would like to read them someday. Kind of like a legacy."

Her daughter's idea touched her heart. Betsy had created so many lasting memories for Annie, now she had the opportunity to do the same for her grandchildren, connecting the generations with her words. "What a wonderful idea."

"I thought so."

"And here I'm always bragging about my clever daughter."

"As if you have a choice?"

They laughed together.

"Are you planning on staying there indefinitely?"

Annie heard the worry in her daughter's voice and tried to ignore the tug in her chest. LeeAnn didn't want to admit that Annie was making a place for herself here in Stony Point. A place so far away from her home in Texas.

In Texas Annie had been alone. Not lonely, since she had friends and kept herself busy, but alone just the same. Maybe it had been the empty house. The memory of Wayne, and their life together, shadowed her days. LeeAnn had a full life—the responsibilities and antics of her children and the companionship of her husband. She didn't see the empty void in Annie's life. And Annie would never burden her daughter by complaining.

Stony Point had opened up a new chapter for Annie. Just like a good book, she didn't know where the journey was going, but she wasn't ready stop the adventure just yet.

"Maybe after I discover what this Betsy Original means I'll know better what I'm doing. Right now I'm not making any firm plans."

"Just remember you always have a family back here who loves you."

Tears of affection moistened Annie's eyelids. No matter where she went, she had people in her life who loved her. They would always be there for her.

Her throat grew raspy. "As if I could ever forget."

LeeAnn said goodbye, and Annie continued to stare out the window. She missed her family, but ...

Thinking she saw someone moving by the bushes out back, Annie squinted harder. With the deep shadows of twilight having settled in, she couldn't tell if it was a play of the light or her imagination. When nothing stirred again, she shook her head. Obviously, Mr. Smith's arrival had her on high alert. The least little thing had Annie second-guessing herself. One fact was for sure: This mystery was definitely getting to her.

*   *   *   *

At the next Hook and Needle Club, Annie clapped as Alice walked in, giving Alice all the credit for finding the last scene.

"Thank you." Alice took a long sweeping bow. "Thank you very much."

Of course Annie had called Mary Beth right after Alice's discovery, and Mary Beth called the others. Each one had taken the time to drive by the house since then so they could compare notes, but this was the first chance they'd had to get together in person.

"We still don't know what meaning this house holds." Annie handed the picture of the cross-stitch scene to Gwendolyn. "Any idea who the original owner was?"

Gwendolyn shook her head and passed the picture on to Kate. "No. That house was there when I was a girl. I don't remember anything about it." Her brow puckered in thought. "The town records would most likely have that information. We could check there."

"And it just so happens that we have a friend at the town hall," Alice reminded them. "I'm sure the mayor would be more than happy to help. Again."

"He did say he loves digging up information about Stony Point." Annie hesitated to bother the man, but they could use his help once again. "I'll give him a call."

"Your grandmother sure had a way of drawing you into the world she created with her needlework." Kate examined the photo and smiled. "I would love to live in the house or a magical place like it."

Peggy glanced up from stitching her fabric. "Trouble with your ex again?"

"He's trying to make Vanessa choose between us." Kate's cheeks grew red. "It doesn't help that Harry just bought her a new cell phone and drops by out of the blue. I'm trying to teach her to be responsible, which makes me the bad guy while Harry can do no wrong."

Alice dropped down into a chair. "That's just wrong."

"That's why I asked Vanessa to come in a couple hours a day to help out," Mary Beth told them as she tidied up the shop. "We taught her to quilt years ago, so I have her working with the teen class. She's a natural."

A smile crossed Kate's features. "She's stoked, to use her word, about working, and the hours are good. She doesn't have to get up too early, and she never misses time with her friends. A teenager's dream job."

The women laughed at Kate's accurate depiction.

"I remember those days." Alice sighed wistfully. "If it weren't for Annie, I'd probably never have gotten into any really good trouble."

"Hey!"

"It's true. You loved to get into mischief."

"That's why my grandmother always had lists of things to keep me busy."

"Which you always managed to get out of if the day was sunny and you had an idea in mind."

"Like what?" Kate asked, clearly intrigued. "Just so I know what to watch out for with Vanessa."

Alice's face grew animated as she got ready to rat out her friend. "One summer, Betsy got Annie hooked on beads, you know, making bracelets, earrings, that sort of thing. Betsy paid us to clean the entire first floor of Grey Gables until every surface shined. With the money we earned, she drove us to Portland to a craft store full of beads and accessories. We spent hours designing and making all this wonderful jewelry. Then we promised Betsy we'd sell it and give half the profits to the church summer camp."

"Alice—" Annie warned, knowing where Alice headed with this story.

"It's history now. It must be told."

Annie rolled her eyes and took her seat. Despite her mock objection, she enjoyed hearing Alice tell stories about their youth.

"So we're on our way to town to set up a table in the Town Square—"

"You can't do that without a permit," Gwendolyn cut in.

"—thinking we were going to make a fortune, which really, after parts and labor, wasn't much, but we were excited. And at the time, we didn't know we needed a permit. We probably wouldn't have gotten one anyway."

"Then you surely would have been arrested."

"At twelve?" Alice glanced over at Annie. "That would have been fun."

Annie shook her head, a smile playing at the corner of her lips. "Just finish the story."

"On the way, Betsy asked us to stop at a friend's house to deliver a pie she'd baked—blueberry or raspberry, I don't know, some kind of berry. Anyway, lo and behold, there's a birthday party going on. We were asked to stay and the topic of our bead jewelry came up and the next thing you know, Annie is giving it all away."

"They really liked it."

"There went our profits. We had nothing to give to the church program."

Kate laughed. "So what happened?"

"Since we didn't have the money, Betsy made us volunteer at the camp. We worked for two weeks straight." Alice grinned. "But we ended up having fun. A lot more fun than just handing the money over. All because kind-hearted Annie wanted to share."

"What can I say? I'm a soft touch."

Mary Beth patted Annie on the shoulder as she walked by. "And I bet your grandchildren are grateful for that."

"Much to my daughter's displeasure."

"That's what we grandmothers do." Gwendolyn added

her view on the subject. "It's our turn to spoil."

"I'm glad my mother spoils," Peggy told the group. "My daughter gets the extras I can't afford to buy her right now."

"Well, I don't want Vanessa spoiled," Kate said, her tone serious until a small smile emerged. "Well, not too much," she added as she walked to the counter.

"Vanessa is a hard worker. Don't worry about her," Mary Beth assured her.

The women continued to talk about family as the door opened, and Jason hesitantly stepped in.

"Jason?" Mary Beth met him at the door. "Is Stella all right?"

"Fine, just fine. Dictating orders like usual." He smiled at the circle of women. "Look, uh, I stopped by to bring you a message. Seems Mrs. Brickson has a woman from the Museum of Fine Arts in Boston coming to town in a few weeks. She wants to get an opinion on her new cultural center."

"She's really going through with it," Peggy said more than asked.

"Looks that way. Listen, I came by to ask a favor. I don't know what happened, Ms. Brickson won't say, but you've all been friends for a long time. I'm just asking you to be patient with her. It really looks like the cultural center will happen this time."

The women took turns glancing at each other. The normally gregarious man seemed a bit nervous in this decidedly female atmosphere.

"Good for Stella," Mary Beth told him. "And thank you for stopping by to let us know."

"Oh, and Jason, if you want to stick around," Alice grinned, "there's a quilting class about to start."

He backed to the door. "Sorry, not my thing, ladies. I'll just be leaving."

Before he had a chance to grab the doorknob, the door swung in, nearly hitting him. Vanessa breezed in, all smiles, flowing long hair and trendy teen outfit of a summer tank, crop pants, and flip-flops.

"Hey, Jason," she greeted him.

"Morning. I was just leaving." And with that, he high-tailed it from the store.

"What did you do to him?" Vanessa asked the room in general.

"Threatened to enroll him in your quilting class," her mother told her.

Vanessa raised an eyebrow. "I doubt the girls would like that."

"Neither did Jason," Alice deadpanned. "That's why he left in such a hurry."

"That's cool." Vanessa walked behind the counter to place her purse, before moving into the interior of the store. "Anything you want me to do before class?" she asked Mary Beth.

"Yes. Tell us where you got those cute jeans."

Vanessa looked down at her denim crop pants. "At the mall."

"How different." Annie rose from her chair and crossed the room to admire the pants. "I love the crochet on the cuff and the matching belt."

"My mom did that."

Annie looked over at a blushing Kate.

"It was nothing," Kate told her.

"Nothing? Ladies, take a look at this."

At the hem of the cuff, Kate had used ecru classic crochet thread in a scallop pattern. With the same thread, she'd crocheted a matching belt in a lacy floral pattern that   Vanessa had knotted low, leaving the long ends to trail down her leg. The effect was stunning and stylish at the same time.

"I am seriously envious of your talent," Annie told her.

"Thanks." Kate smiled.

Annie glanced at Mary Beth. "You've got a real winner here."

Mary Beth nodded. "That's what I keep telling her. If only she'd listen."

"Some of my friends want her to do their pants," Vanessa said as she walked over to hug her mom. "Of course, being the super mom that she is, she said yes."

"After my paying jobs," Kate said. "I reminded you last night."

"Oh, c'mon," Vanessa pushed. "It won't take that long. I promised."

"Vanessa, we talked about this. I have to work."

"You always have to work," she groused. "I liked it better when you stayed home."

"You know, Kate," Alice interrupted what was about to become a mother-daughter argument, "you could have your own little cottage industry going here."

"I told you that too, Mom."

"I can't charge your friends."

"Sure you can. I would. They've got tons of money."

Annie grimaced. She remembered the hurtful barbs of teenage candor. It was obvious that Kate felt the financial burden of raising her daughter, yet there seemed to be some residual guilt in Kate's eyes. She had a tough job ahead of her.

Alice nodded. "Spoken like a true entrepreneur."

"I don't know…" Kate started to say.

"It's a great way to start a money-making venture," Annie told her. "And there's nothing like shaping your own destiny."

"I second that." Alice grew serious as she regarded Kate. "Just think about it," she urged her.

Kate held up her hands in defense. "Okay. I'll think about it." She pointed to Vanessa. "We'll talk later."

"I've heard that before." Vanessa rolled her eyes before turning to Annie. "Mom said you found another clue to your mystery lady."

"Yes. Now all four scenes have been discovered, but we're still no closer to figuring out who the young woman in the cross-stitch is."

"Bummer."

"I couldn't have said it better."

"What do we do now?" Peggy asked.

"Honestly, I'm stumped." Annie returned to her chair. "But I owe you all so much for helping me."

"Are you kidding?" Mary Beth joined the circle. "We've been thrilled to help."

"In that case, thank you all." Annie took a deep breath and announced her next step in the cross-stitch saga. "I think it's time to bring the cross-stitch here to the shop."

"Thank goodness." Gwendolyn dropped her knitting in her lap. "I thought you'd never let us see it in person! I mean, it's a little tough to solve a mystery when we haven't personally seen the scenes in question up close and personal."

Annie felt bad about that, but she hadn't been able to let go. Hadn't been able to shed her fear that once the piece was out of her hands, she'd lose what little control she had in this whole endeavor. Now, with the scenes discovered, she realized, ready or not, it was time. "I'm afraid I've been a little selfish about sharing the Betsy Original. It's such a link between Betsy and me."

"We understand." Mary Beth's eyes glistened. "But we are thrilled to finally see it in person."

Kate clasped her hands together over her chest. "I can't wait. This has got to be the highlight of the summer."

"Then it's a date," Annie told them. "You finally get to meet the Lady."

— 16 —

Later that afternoon, after a quick bite to eat, Annie went to the living room to tackle the next remodeling task on her list. She and Alice had chosen a soft sea-green paint for the walls, and Annie planned on prepping the room so she could start painting tomorrow. As she lifted the Lady in the Attic to carry it into the library for safe keeping, her gaze fell to the little house scene. They'd found the house, yes, but like the other scenes, not the significance behind it. So really they hadn't fully uncovered the clues. Why were they having such a hard time understanding what tied the various scenes together?

After setting up the frame and returning the piece to its place, she got an urge to call Ian. He'd been helpful with the storefront, maybe he could find out who originally owned the house.

She crossed to the desk and the purse she'd dumped there earlier, searching for the card with Ian's work number. She paused for a moment. Even though Ian had given her his work number and encouraged her to call, she didn't want him to think she was a nuisance, only using him for information—when in fact she sort of was. No, change that to asking a friend for a favor. "He's a nice guy," she muttered to Boots, who had just jumped onto the window seat to take yet another nap in the sunlight.

"He said to call if I need anything, so call." After arguing with herself, she finally punched the numbers. Her call went right through.

"Annie, you're still in town," he said instead of hello.

"Imagine that. No one's asked to me leave."

"After the last conversation we had ..."

"No one's bothered me since, Ian."

"Good to hear it." Annie heard papers rustle on the other end. "What can I help you with today?"

"I have good news, actually. Alice found the house from the scene on the cross-stitch. But none of the Hook and Needle members can recall who originally lived there, especially since it's changed owners several times through the years. I thought maybe you could help us out again."

"You have a team working on the mystery now?"

"There was no avoiding it."

He laughed. "I can understand why. Your grandmother made this hard to resist."

"Can you help?"

"Sure, where is this house?"

She gave him the address.

"I have some pressing issues that I have to deal with, so give me a few days."

Annie hated to wait that long, but she couldn't push him. He was generous enough to help, but he had a job to do and that came first.

"I know you've heard this before, but I really appreciate your help, Ian."

"Actually, I'm glad to help."

After saying goodbye, Annie stared at the cross-stitch

for a long moment. "We're getting closer," she whispered to the Lady in the Attic, if only to convince herself.

*   *   *   *

Tuesday dawned with a slight mist that continued into the early morning. Annie had driven to Magruder's Groceries for string to secure the covering for the Betsy Original. She'd hoped for a better day to transport the piece and got her wish as the sun burst through the mass of gray clouds on her return home. Happy that she didn't have to worry about inclement weather after all, she hummed as she walked up the path to the porch. Keys still in hand, she unlocked and pushed the front door open and nearly tripped over Boots as she streaked out of the house.

"Hey! Slow down there." Usually the cat only moved that fast when there was food involved.

Shaking her head, she entered and closed the door. Just in time to see a dark shape looming in the hallway.

"W-what?" she stuttered, dropping her purse.

The figure dropped a large object, then ran into the kitchen. Annie heard the back door slam.

It took several moments to get her wits about her. When she did, she rushed toward the object, now recognizing it as the framed Betsy Original. She picked it up and carried it back into the library before running to the kitchen. The door was partially open. Annie looked outside but didn't see the intruder. She closed and locked the door, leaning back against it to catch her breath and slow her heart rate. "This is getting very scary," she whispered.

Her heart jumped against her chest minutes later when a knock sounded at the front door, followed by the doorbell. Cautiously, Annie moved to the living room to covertly peek out the window. Relief overwhelmed her when she saw Alice standing on the porch.

"What took so long?" Alice asked when Annie finally let her in.

"You wouldn't believe me if I told you."

Alice's expression turned grave as she viewed Annie's face. "What's wrong?"

"Someone tried to steal the Lady."

Alice's eyes grew wide. "Excuse me?"

"I had to run down to Magruder's Groceries, and when I got back, there was someone in the hallway holding the Betsy Original. I startled him, and he ran off."

"We need to call the police."

"I intended to, just as soon as I pulled myself together."

Alice marched to the kitchen and picked up the phone to punch in a number. Annie assumed it was the police department. She was glad Alice took control. Her shaking fingers wouldn't have accomplished much.

Fifteen minutes later, an officer arrived at Grey Gables. Annie assured the young man that she was fine, then gave a statement, including a description of Roger Smith, the man who had been asking about purchasing the Betsy Original. The officer looked over the hallway and went to check the back door, eventually rejoining the ladies. He promised to drive by the house while on patrol. Annie told him the Betsy Original would be at A Stitch in Time after today. He made a note of that before going outside to take a last look around the perimeter of the house.

"Are you sure you're fine?" Alice asked her for the tenth time.

"Now I am," Annie assured her.

"Do you still want to go to A Stitch in Time? I'm sure the others would understand if you canceled."

"Actually, I think the Original will probably be safer there. Mary Beth must have a store security system. I could leave the piece there for the time being."

"Good idea."

"Let's not say anything about this. I don't want them spooked."

"Annie—"

"Just for the time being."

"Okay," Alice replied, her tone less than sure.

"Let's get the Lady wrapped up."

They went to the library. Annie replaced the muslin wrapping she'd draped over the piece before the intruder had removed it. Alice folded a thick blanket securely around the frame while Annie made sure the bundle was safely fastened together. Despite the fact that she knew the piece wasn't safe here at Grey Gables, she had a hard time actually wrapping it for delivery. An odd foreboding nagged at her, as if the events of the day weren't the end to this crazy turn of events. *Probably just nerves*, she thought, but couldn't be sure. Still, she couldn't back out. She'd made a promise to her friends and had to follow through.

"This is going to make the girls crazy," Alice said as she stepped away from the frame. "Covering the piece in total secrecy until the official unveiling."

"Think of it like Christmas morning."

"That should work."

Annie hoped so.

Just before eleven they arrived at the store. The Hook and Needle Club waited by the door, anticipating their entrance.

"We can't wait to see it," Mary Beth laughed, her unwavering gaze darting directly to the large, covered frame.

"At least let us get in the door," Alice groused as she and Annie carried the bundle inside and set the framed piece on the counter for safekeeping until they removed the outer covering. "At this rate, we may not let you see what's underneath."

Peggy glared at her. "Alice MacFarlane, you're just plain mean. And a showoff. You've already seen the Lady."

"You would make us wait?" Gwendolyn demanded.

"Alice is just playing with you." Annie scanned the interior of the shop to see where Mary Beth had set up the display easel. "Don't you think we should wait for Stella?"

Peggy glanced at her watch. "She's usually here by now."

"I called her to tell her about the unveiling," Mary Beth told the group, a look of regret saddening her face. "I don't think she's coming."

Annie ignored the piercing disappointment. Maybe she hadn't gained any ground by hoping Stella would come and look, but they had to move on. "In that case, the uncovering is the first item on our agenda."

"We have an agenda?" Kate asked, confusion wrinkling her brow.

"We're a club, right? We must have a plan." Annie looked at Mary Beth. "Don't we?"

"Have you noticed one so far?"

"Well, no."

Alice came up behind Annie and grinned over her shoulder. "Ms. Detail is all about lists and organization. Don't hold it against her."

"The only thing I'm going to hold against anyone," Mary Beth announced, "is time we're wasting."

"Then I shouldn't torture you any longer." Annie strolled to the frame to remove the outer blanket. She left the muslin in place. "I don't know," she said, her brows angled together in feigned concern. "Maybe we should work on our projects first."

"Annie," Mary Beth warned.

"Okay." She laughed as she and Alice loosened the muslin before placing the frame on the easel. Once they were sure it was secure, Annie grabbed two ends of the muslin to snatch it away. "Ta-da."

Gasps followed by total silence.

"My reaction, exactly," Alice whispered to the women.

As a group, they all moved forward to view the Lady more closely.

Mary Beth spoke up first. "As usual, her stitching is flawless."

"The detail." Gwendolyn slipped on her glasses. "Very lifelike. I've never seen anything like it."

"I've always envied her talent, but this makes it official."

Annie moved close and placed a hand on Kate's shoulder. "Don't ever be envious. You have your own special talent."

Kate glanced at Annie, eyes welling up. "Thanks," she whispered.

The ladies shifted position to inspect the handiwork.

Annie stood back with Alice to watch their reactions. After a good fifteen minutes of oohing and ahhing, Annie insisted they sit down and get back to the task of working on their own projects.

"We have a treasure here," Gwendolyn told Annie. "Your grandmother outdid herself on this piece."

"You really wonder what the Lady was thinking about," Kate remarked. "What was going on in her life? It looks like a happy place and time."

"But does anyone recognize her?" Annie asked.

They shook their heads.

"Not any more in person than in the snapshots you took," Mary Beth said.

"I was afraid of that."

"I'm not one to get all sentimental—"

"Really, Peggy," Alice teased. "Do tell."

"But that woman must have really meant something to your grandmother. You can tell she worked hard to bring that across."

"That's what I thought too."

Gwendolyn nodded. "The hours she would have put into it."

"And knowing Betsy, it was time well spent." Mary Beth stood in front of the frame. "I can just imagine her working into the small hours of the night, striving to get this finished."

"A labor of love," Gwendolyn agreed.

"And unless we know who the woman is, we'll never know why my grandmother stitched it."

"You know, there is a way to solve that dilemma."

All eyes moved to Mary Beth.

"Spill," Alice told her.

"We feature it at A Stitch in Time. I'll e-mail my customers that we're going to show a new Betsy Original. Make a call to the president of the New England Stitch Club with viewing dates. We'll be swamped."

Annie hesitated. "I don't know if that's what Betsy had in mind." Or if she wanted Mary Beth to be in danger by housing the piece here.

"Betsy was always generous about sharing her work." Alice reached over and patted her hand. "You never know what might happen by showing the piece. Someone might recognize her."

Gwendolyn's needles clicked as she knitted. "Your grandmother left you a gift, Annie. There's no way to know what her intent was because she didn't leave you instructions, but she must have trusted your judgment." She stopped, looked around the group. "Like we do."

Like we do. Three little words, but words that meant the world to Annie. Words she was thrilled to hear. She'd wanted to fit in, hoped she would, and Gwendolyn's words about trust confirmed it. Still, could she let Gram's work go? Her own personal link to a woman who had given her so much, taught her so much? Did she want to share it with the world?

Though she didn't have an answer to all those questions, she knew one thing for certain. She really wanted— no, needed—to find the identity of the woman in the cross-stitch. Maybe displaying it was the only way to find out.

Oh, Gram, I wish I knew what to do.

"We aren't going to twist your arm," Mary Beth assured her. "But knowing Betsy like I did, I don't think she'd mind. After all, she had lots of work on display in her life."

Which begged the question, why had this particular piece been hidden in the attic? And who wanted it so badly they would try to steal it?

Annie looked at these women, these friends. She knew that they wouldn't steer her wrong. At least she hoped they wouldn't.

"You know this is a big deal for me."

"Yeah, we do," Alice told her in a gentle voice.

The club hour went by quickly, with the women still admiring the Lady in the Attic and reminiscing about Betsy. By the time they'd all gathered up their projects for the day, ready to say good-bye, Annie needed reassurance.

"Allowing public access to the piece will be a good thing, right?"

Alice rolled her eyes. "That's what we've been trying to tell you."

"And that's what I've been trying to accept."

Peggy opened the door. "We're leaving now, so your final answer is?"

Gwendolyn swatted at Peggy. "Give the girl a minute."

Mary Beth groaned. "We've given her lots of minutes. Sixty to be exact."

"Which I appreciate. I've made up my mind."

Kate grinned. "She's going to say yes."

"How could you possibly—"

"Peggy!"

"All right. I'll be quiet."

Kate continued with her original thought. "Because she has that look."

"The look that says ..." Mary Beth waved her hand in a circular motion to urge Annie on.

She couldn't keep them in suspense any longer. She had to commit. It was now or never. Making a mental note to tell Mary Beth about the intruder at Grey Gables earlier that morning so she could take precautions with the Lady, Annie said, "The look that says ... yes."

Amid claps and relieved laugher, Alice shook her head. "I couldn't have prolonged that any better if I tried." She flashed a heartfelt grin at her friend. "The list of reasons why I'm glad you're here keeps getting longer."

"You've certainly added a much needed shot of life to our club," Mary Beth said, hugging Annie.

Even if she hadn't meant to.

～ 17 ～

Word soon got out about the revealing of a post-humous Betsy Original. And, much to Annie's chagrin, the fact that someone had tried to steal it from Grey Gables. The notoriety created a steady stream of customers pouring through A Stitch in Time. Everyone was eager to view what was being billed as Betsy's greatest work, and also to buy needlecraft items. For three weeks now, Mary Beth had walked around with a huge smile on her face, clearly in her element. Kate, on the other hand, worked more hours, with the perk of being able to display her hand-crocheted jackets. When Annie came by for the regular Tuesday morn-ing Hook and Needle Club, Kate looked worn out.

"You've been busy?"

"Crazy is more like it. Who knew how big this would be?"

Yeah, who knew? Standing across the room from the framed cross-stitch, Annie couldn't help but feel as though she'd lost a bit of control in her own life. The piece was a hit, but no one recognized the young woman. Annie had gotten used to sitting in her quiet living room to gaze at the piece; now she had to come downtown to the shop and stand in line. She felt like her grandkids with a toy they didn't want to share, tempted to stomp her foot and say "mine" and bring it back home to Grey Gables. But she'd made a commitment and would keep her word.

Gwendolyn emitted a groan behind Annie. "I guess we'll have to cancel the club today. There's nowhere to sit."

Annie turned. "Not only that, with all the commotion, I don't think we'd get much done anyway."

"Then let's do something else." Gwendolyn hooked her arm through Annie's and drew her outside. "I know just the thing."

Thinking they would end up at The Cup & Saucer like everyone else, Annie was surprised when they passed the diner and headed to the end of the block, crossed the street, and stopped outside a recently renovated storefront. Through the windows Annie could make out a small construction crew. And none other than Stella.

"The new cultural center?"

"When it's ready. Stella called John last night for advice about her newest financial venture. He was amused because Stella has plenty of family money for this project of hers. I think she wanted John to pass the news on to me without having to actually talk to me."

Taking hold of the door handle, Gwendolyn went inside with Annie on her heels.

Stella, with her back to them, barked out orders like a commander in battle. She glanced at her watch. "I have one hour, gentlemen. Snap to."

Before Stella noticed them, Annie surveyed the vast, open room. The dark wooden floors had been buffed to a bright sheen. The scent of fresh paint permeated the room. Two men worked on installing track lighting while the other assembled recessed shelving.

"My, my, you are the busy one," Gwendolyn said as Stella turned on her heel, stunned to see them.

Her hand flew to her chest. "I didn't hear you come in."

"With all the instruction-giving, I imagine not." Gwendolyn nodded in approval. "This old storefront is turning out wonderful. Your cultural center will be a hit."

Stella glanced around, as if seeing the space through the eyes of others. "Do you think so?"

"Most definitely. Very professional," Gwendolyn said. "How about a tour?"

"There isn't much to see right now, but this is it."

Stella hesitated to say more as she looked at Annie out of the corner of her eye. "You're here now. You might as well know what's going on."

With that said, she explained that the main open room would house the exhibits she hoped to showcase. The reception desk hadn't arrived yet, but would be placed strategically by the front door. There would be display tables set up as soon as she had inventory. There were two offices in the back, as well as a small kitchenette and bathroom.

"So this is the tour," Stella said as she finished. "It was slow going at first since I've been working alone, but it's finally all come together."

"I thought you had help."

Stella's eyes darted away momentarily. "I did initially. My new board has been a great help, but the women all had other commitments. I needed the work done by today."

"Today? What have you planned?" Gwendolyn pressed.

"A dear friend from the Museum of Fine Arts in Boston is vacationing in the area. I asked her to stop by and give me her input." A panicked look crossed Stella's face. "She'll be here in an hour and I'm not ready."

"What can we do to help?" Annie asked.

Stella's brows rose. "Oh, no, you don't need to do anything."

"Stella, you're our friend. We want to help."

"But, really, I—"

"Stella," Annie pressed. "We want to do this for you."

Surprised again, Stella's tense features softened. She looked to Annie as though seeing her for who she really was for the first time.

"Well, we could get rid of all these boxes and tidy up."

Gwendolyn saluted. "We'll get right on it."

For the next hour Annie and Gwendolyn took orders, along with the rest of the workmen, as they finished their tasks. They'd just stowed away the broom and placed the empty boxes in the dumpster when the door opened and a tall, thin woman in her late forties walked in. She was dressed in tailored taupe Bermuda shorts and a loose-fitting blouse, her blond hair cut in a stylish bob.

"Stella. It's been too long."

Stella hurried over to greet her friend. "Marisa, I'm so pleased you could make the time to stop by."

"Or miss seeing your plans? Never." Marisa air-kissed Stella, then gazed around the room.

Marisa sauntered around the open room with a critical eye, commenting on the lighting, the acoustics, even the shade of paint on the walls. And the entire time Stella stayed rooted to one spot, worry lining her face, as if she were afraid to engage with Marisa for fear she might find some fault in Stella's design.

Annie would have liked to walk over and placed a comforting hand on Stella's shoulder. She didn't, knowing the older woman wouldn't appreciate her gesture.

After a final assessment full of hmms and aahs, Marisa smiled brightly. "The space is wonderful. You thought of everything when you set up the exhibit area."

Stella let out a breath of relief. "I'm so glad you agree."

Marisa wagged a finger at her friend. "I always said you were very clever, Stella."

As if suddenly remembering Annie and Gwendolyn, Stella introduced them to Marisa. "These are my friends."

Annie's eyes widened at her statement.

"We're all members of a local needlecraft club."

Before Annie could add to Stella's introduction, Marisa came over to shake her hand.

"How lovely," Marisa told her. "I have a special place in my heart for needlecrafts. After I return home from vacation, I'm finalizing a new exhibit set to open in October: Celebrate Americana. It will include different textiles and modes of needlecraft that women have worked through the years."

"Oh, then, you must stop by our local yarn shop before you leave town," Gwendolyn told her. "We have a group of women, including Stella, who get together and work on different needlecraft projects. In fact, there's a new, never-before-seen Betsy Original being displayed there right now."

Marisa stopped. A glint of anticipation, as well as calculation, was in her eyes. "A new Betsy Original?"

"Yes. It's beautiful."

Annie watched Stella's reaction. Her lips pursed in impatience and her bearing grew stiff as Gwendolyn described the cross-stitch.

"Where did it come from?" asked Marisa.

"I found it," Annie told her. "Betsy was my grandmother, and I inherited her house. I'm spending the summer here and found it in the attic."

"You really should see it," Gwendolyn said with all seriousness.

Marisa smiled at Stella. "Have you been holding out on me, my friend?"

"Well, I—"

"Stella, you have a Betsy Original in town. Let's check it out. Then I'll share my ideas for your exhibit space."

Annie picked up her purse. "Let's go."

The four walked to the store, Marisa and Gwendolyn taking the lead, chatting like long-lost friends. Stella walked silently beside Annie, who slowed to the older woman's pace. She'd have no choice but to see the cross-stitch now. Annie didn't know how Stella would respond, especially since she was only going at Marisa's request.

As they entered the shop, Stella lingered by the door until Marisa took her arm and led her to the display stand. Annie held back far enough to be out of Stella's way, but close enough to watch her reaction.

Eyes narrowed, lips taut, Stella stepped up to the cross-stitch. At first, she looked all around the store, at anything but the image. Finally, she gazed directly at the cloth. Initially nothing registered; then, slowly, her eyes grew wide.

By this time Mary Beth had engaged Marisa in conversation, but Stella stayed motionless. Then, reaching out, her fingers lightly brushed the cloth before covering her mouth. A small cry escaped her.

Concerned, Annie stepped toward her just as Stella

turned. Tears streamed down Stella's face, her eyes filled with … regret? Loss? Annie couldn't name the emotion.

Stella's gaze met and held hers for moments. Then she took a deep breath, straightened her shoulders, and brushed past Annie. By the time Annie realized what was happening, Stella had disappeared into the storeroom at the back of the shop.

Weaving her way through customers, Annie felt someone grab her arm. She turned to see Marisa. "We need to talk. I want to show this piece in the new exhibit."

Annie stared at her for a moment. "What?"

"I want to show this piece."

"Oh, I can't do that."

"Of course you can."

All Annie could concentrate on right now was Stella. "Please excuse me."

Annie barreled through the room, only to run into Ian.

"Hey," he said. "I was hoping to bump into you."

She didn't need a distraction right now. She had to get to Stella. "Ian, I don't mean to be rude, but can it wait?"

"Sure. I'll be here."

In the storeroom, Annie found Stella, who had stopped to catch her breath and staggered to a desk chair. She was fishing through her purse to find a tissue.

Alarm flittered through Annie. "Stella? Are you okay?"

Clearing her throat, Stella turned, clenching a ball of tissue in one hand as she visibly tried to maintain her composure. "Annie. You shouldn't have followed me."

"I wanted to make sure you're okay."

"I'm fine, as you can see."

"You don't look fine to me."

"Well I am. You can go now."

"No. I'm afraid I can't. Not until I get answers. You know the Lady in the cross-stitch, don't you?"

Stella placed a hand over her chest. "Why would you say that?"

"Because you're the only person I've seen have such an emotional reaction to the piece."

"I can't help you."

"Can't or won't?"

"I'm sorry," she said, voice firm, stubbornly signaling the end of the conversation.

Annie began to pace in the confined space. "All this time we've been going out of our minds trying to figure out what this cross-stitch piece means. If you'd looked at it from the start like we asked, you could have given us the answers."

"You're assuming I knew her."

"I know you did. Your reaction says so."

Stella's voice grew acerbic. "Maybe some truths are better left unanswered."

"Better for whom?"

"If your grandmother had wanted the young lady's identity known, she would have told you."

"Stella, we've all worked so hard to find out who the woman is. We've gone to the places that must have meant something to my grandmother, searching for the truth behind Gram's work. If you know anything at all, please, tell me." Annie didn't bother to hide the frustration on her face. "Why won't you tell me?"

"Because the young woman is me."

～ 18 ～

Stella smiled sadly. "From a long time ago."

"Oh my," Annie whispered.

"Oh my, indeed."

Just as Annie was about to ask how and why, Mary Beth rapped on the door frame. "Hey, you two, I saw you run back here and—" She stopped abruptly when she glimpsed Annie's dazed expression. Her gaze quickly flew to Stella's pale face. "Is everything okay?" Mary Beth asked with alarm.

Annie looked at Stella, her brow raised in silent question. Stella clutched her purse tighter and hugged it to her chest, then nodded.

"Mary Beth, would you gather together the Hook and Needle Club members?" She paused. "Stella and I want to tell you something."

Mary Beth hesitated a half second. "Of course."

After Mary Beth left the room, Annie heard her loudly announce that the shop must briefly close. Everyone would be welcome back in an hour. She directed customers—even Marisa—to The Cup & Saucer, down to the Town Square, the park, or the docks to view the lobster boats.

Stella looked up at Annie. "I don't know where to start."

"At the beginning would be good."

Stella's lips curved slightly. "You're very much like Betsy, you know."

"So I've been told."

Minutes later Mary Beth returned. "All clear. I ran everyone out."

Annie took hold of Stella's elbow, slowly leading her into the outer room. Stella's color had returned, but Annie wasn't taking a chance that Stella, frail as she was, might crumble before she reached the circle of chairs.

Once Stella was comfortably seated, Annie sat beside her and motioned for the others to join them. As in their Tuesday-morning meetings, the solidarity of friendship was strengthened as they sat in the circle.

Stella took a deep breath. "I know the identity of the young woman in the cross-stitch."

The announcement had them speechless. Finally, Alice asked, "Well?"

Stella bowed her head.

Five confused faces stared at her.

Annie's heart went out to the woman. She waited for Stella to gain her composure. When Stella raised her head, Annie nodded at Stella.

When she hesitated, Annie took charge. "We all know the woman." Annie shifted in her seat. "She's sitting at the head of this circle."

A hushed silence fell over the group, but as the revelation sank in, Alice whispered, "Stella?"

Questions flew fast and furious. Stella held up her hand to deflect them. "Yes, it's me. I didn't know I was the young lady in the piece. Today is the first time I saw it—believe me, I'm as surprised as you."

"But how? Why?" Peggy stammered.

Stella clutched the armrests as if holding on to a lifeline. "It's a long story."

"And we aren't going anywhere until it's been told," Mary Beth assured her. "I locked the front door and turned the closed sign so no one will disturb us."

Stella paused a moment, meeting each woman eye to eye, as if to convince them that the real Stella, not the façade she'd always hidden behind, spoke to them now. "My mother died when I was very young. We had lived in the house on Old Harbor Road. That stitching in the corner of the cross-stitch? That was my home."

"I didn't know you lived there," Gwendolyn interrupted. "You never mentioned it."

"When I was about twelve, my father moved us to a bigger house, outside of town. All for status, you know." Stella shrugged, but the forced disdain in her tone revealed this was not a minor detail. "Now I was even more isolated than before. And miserable. The only company I had were the many books my father insisted I read. He believed in having his only child tutored at home, so I had no friends to speak of. Until I met this outgoing girl in town when I accompanied the cook to the market one day. Having a friend to talk to changed my life."

"Betsy," Kate deduced.

"Yes. I had wandered off by myself, curious about the places in town I wasn't allowed to visit. I ended up at the ducks that afternoon. Betsy was there with a few others, leading the younger children in a game of tag or some other children's game. I watched from the sidelines, afraid to dirty my new dress. Once she noticed me, a big smile broke out, and she dragged me into the game. She asked my name, introduced me, and before I knew it, I was included in the group as one of their own."

Annie smiled. "My grandmother never let anyone stand alone. She pulled others into her life whether they wanted it or not."

"And I didn't. Not at first. This was all new to me. I didn't even go to school in town, and here I was, running around the docks with children I'd never met, yet they acted like this was normal. I was as scared as I was excited. What would my father think?" Stella smoothed her skirt, a smile softening her features. "Before long Betsy and I became inseparable. Although she was five years older than I, age didn't matter. We did everything together. She became the family I desperately wanted since my father had taken to traveling by then. I barely saw him."

"Let me guess. You were adopted by my grandmother's family?"

"Yes." Stella visibly relaxed as the words tumbled from her. "I probably spent more time in your great-grandmother's kitchen than in my own. It was a special time, one I've never forgotten." She laughed. "I can still smell the homemade cookies whenever I think about those times."

"It must have been heaven on earth for you." Alice grinned in camaraderie. "I know that's how I felt when Betsy would get me out of my house to visit her after my divorce."

"And I'll bet she had you involved in a needlework project," Mary Beth added.

Stella smiled. "Even back then Betsy involved her friends in needlework. She taught me everything I know about needlecrafts, which isn't much compared to her. As hard as I tried, I could never be as good as she." The light in Stella's eyes dimmed. "Betsy had a natural flair, a gift, and—God help me—I was always jealous of that."

Ah, Annie thought. *That explains why Stella stuck to her practical knitting.*

"And then one day, handsome, charming Charlie Holden sauntered into our lives and changed everything." Stella's lips straightened into a hard line.

"My grandfather," Annie whispered.

"He swept us off our feet."

"Both of you?" Peggy blurted.

"Yes." Stella's eyes flashed with pain. "But he only had eyes for Betsy."

Annie felt a reluctant tug of sympathy.

"He was nice enough to me at first," said Stella, "and I misinterpreted it as romantic interest. I fell in love and believed he loved me in return. I believed what I wanted so desperately to believe. When he didn't return the sentiment, I was stunned, then hurt. Betsy and Charlie spent more and more time together. When they decided to get married, I was devastated. I blamed Betsy for stealing the man I loved."

"Surely, you realized that wasn't the truth," whispered Alice.

"Not right away. I stayed angry with her, first for her relationship with Charlie, and then because I was afraid of losing the only family I had become a part of. If she married Charlie, what would become of me? I was convinced I was still in love with him, so I lashed out instead of joining Betsy in her newfound happiness. As a young woman, I only felt the pain of their abandonment hitting so close to home, like my mother's passing and my father's only interest being his business. She'd done the one thing that had the power to hurt me, and I couldn't forgive her.

"I begged my father to let me stay with relatives in New York. He agreed and I attended school there, eventually married Seymour and tried to forget about life in Stony Point and the new Mrs. Charlie Holden." Tears brightened her eyes, and her words wavered. "I never spoke to her again."

Annie thought of her grandmother, of the times Annie would ask her to tell family stories. Betsy would laugh and relate a story, but oftentimes, afterward, she'd stare off into the distance, sadness in her eyes. Annie never knew what caused that look. She did now.

"Is that why you wouldn't look at the Betsy Original? Because my grandmother stitched it?"

"I could barely look at your grandmother, let alone her work. And when you talked about this new piece, I had no idea who the woman in the piece was. I only knew that if Betsy stitched it, it would be beautiful, and I wanted no part of it. After all these years, I still couldn't bring myself to set eyes on her work. Partly from my sorrow over the way things ended," Stella paused. "But mostly from guilt. From ruining our friendship. I know I hurt Betsy by my actions."

"She must have understood," Annie assured her.

"When we were younger, yes, but not later."

"Why?" Annie asked, confused.

"Your grandmother had started to show samplings of her work at different venues throughout New England.

Word of her work reached New York, and many scrambled to showcase it."

"But that never happened," Annie said. "My grandmother would have told me if her work was shown in New York. That was her dream."

"It never happened," said Stella. "I stopped it."

Disbelief coursed through Annie.

Stella continued. "I heard your grandmother was coming to New York. I wouldn't see her, and I couldn't allow her be successful in *my* city. A few well-placed telephone calls and a few 'untruths' passed on to the right people, and any hope your grandmother had of showing her work in New York was finished." She paused a moment, her voice a near whisper. "As soon as I'd made the calls, I knew I'd set in motion something I could never take back."

Mary Beth flinched. "Did Betsy ever find out?"

"I don't know."

Annie tamped down her resentment. It had to be difficult for this proud woman to admit all this, not just to Annie, but to her other friends as well. "I know you were hurt, angry even, but she was your friend. Why didn't you try to make amends?"

"I had this crazy notion that Betsy should come to me. After all, it was what I saw as her betrayal of me that got us to that point." Stella's brows knit together. Her hands shook as she steadied herself by fiddling with the clasp of her purse. "I didn't even have that first blush of love with Seymour. I admired him, certainly, but I can't say I was swept off my feet. Not like Betsy and Charlie. It wasn't until we'd been married for many years that I realized I'd grown to love him." Almost defiantly, she added, "We had a good life."

"I've no doubt you did," Gwendolyn assured her.

"I was truly heartbroken when he passed. We never had children, and I was left in a big, empty house in New York trying to make sense of my life. That's when I decided to come back to Maine and never speak of my past life to anyone."

Annie grimaced. "So that no one could hurt you again?"

"That and so I wouldn't reopen the wound of my loss." Years of sadness lined Stella's face. "It's ironic. I never let anyone see the real me, yet that image of me in the cross-stitch bares it all. I've never been inside Grey Gables. Charlie and Betsy bought it after I left town, yet your grandmother stitched me there as if I belonged."

"I'm sure she thought you did." Annie reached over to cover Stella's wrinkled hand with hers. Apparently, her grandmother had forgiven Stella, her last cross-stitch work a worthy testament to that. It was the least Annie could do as well. "My grandmother taught me that life was messy, but regardless of that, you need to live life to the fullest."

"Easy for her to say. She always had a bright outlook on life."

"She did, but she also had her share of sorrow. I have a feeling losing your friendship was one of those sorrows."

"When I came back here, I thought the past wouldn't bother me. It's amazing how you can make yourself believe something if you're stubborn enough." Stella shook her head. "I never had the courage to visit Betsy once I came back. I regret that now."

Gwendolyn's lips curved. "And the cross-stitch is

proof that Betsy still considered you her friend."

"Seeing it has shifted a pattern of my life," Stella told them all. "I hope I can be a different person from now on, thanks to a gift from my old friend."

She glanced at Annie, the glimmer of a wary smile on her lips. "I thought I was doing fine, until you came to the first Hook and Needle Club. I looked at you but saw Betsy. And I'm afraid I didn't treat you very kindly."

"Leaving me to wonder what I'd done to you."

"After Betsy passed, I realized I could no longer ignore the past, but I still didn't take steps to move on. Meeting you jolted me into reality."

"I suppose my showing up was a bit of a shock."

"Especially when you joined our club. I'm afraid I stubbornly hung onto the belief that if I didn't engage you, the past couldn't haunt me." She sniffled. "But it did. I'd let years of bitterness rule my life. Of my own choosing, I missed out on years of happiness. I watched you become part of the town, saw so much of Betsy in you. I finally admitted to myself that I missed Betsy. Only it was too late to do anything about it. So I made matters worse all over again."

"How?"

"I hired Mr. Smith to buy the Betsy Original from you, thinking I could get it, and Betsy's legacy, out of my life again. I'm afraid he took his assignment too seriously. I never, ever meant for him to try to steal it. And I never meant for him to scare you."

"He did scare me, but he didn't hurt me. And after word got out about the botched burglary attempt, he'd have been crazy to hang around and take a chance of getting caught."

"It seems I'm always making the wrong decisions."

Annie smiled. "You can change all that, you know."

Stella shook her head. "It's too late now that Betsy's gone."

"Please," Annie snorted. "It's never too late to make things right."

"And how would I do that?"

"I think you know," Annie whispered.

Stella gazed at Annie. "I'm so sorry for everything. To you. To Betsy."

"There you go," smiled Annie as she patted Stella's hand.

Stella sighed. "You do have a lot of Betsy in you. You have her wisdom and patience. I sensed it the first time I met you."

Warmth unfolded in Annie at the unexpected compliment. Through Annie's entire life, Gram had been an awesome example of grace under pressure. And she thought coming to Stony Point would be difficult, especially with Gram gone. Instead, she'd learned more about her grandmother, more about herself, than she ever imagined. The initial sadness had passed, filled now with joyful memories and a sense of pride in the woman Annie had always respected and loved. She only hoped she could follow in her footsteps.

Up to this point, the other women had been quiet, hanging onto every word as Stella related her story. Now that all of Stella's past had been revealed, the women bombarded her with questions. Stella answered each one, even though her energy had to have been totally drained.

Peggy rose from her chair and crossed to the framed cross-stitch. "I can't stand it any longer. You have got to tell us what the scenes mean."

"That was very clever of Betsy," Stella said as she joined Peggy beside the piece. "But then, Betsy always knew how to create a total picture." She ran her finger lightly over the stitching. "I loved to run barefoot in the sand, but my father didn't want me to muss up my clothes or act unladylike. We found this hidden cove and played there during the summer." She glanced over to the women. "We bought yarn at the store. It was called Five and Dime back then—just Five and Dime."

"I remember my mother talking about that store," Gwendolyn said. "I never knew it was the old Bascom's Department Store."

"During the autumn months, we used to hide up in Betsy's uncle's barn, reading and playing games. I guess that's why she stitched it. She loved sitting in the freshly cut hay." Stella's eyes grew misty. "And of course, my childhood house. I never realized I was so lonely until Betsy came along."

Annie glanced at the circle of women as they stared at the cross-stitch, each lost in her own thoughts. How odd, to have each one of them seated in her usual chair but not working on her needlecraft. Today their joint project was to support a friend.

"I wonder if your grandmother left that cross-stitch in the attic on purpose for you to find," Alice said to Annie.

"I don't think we'll ever know for sure, but my grandmother never did anything without a purpose. Maybe she meant for Stella to find it somehow."

"Well, she did," Gwendolyn exclaimed.

The women laughed and Kate asked, "What happens to the piece now?"

At the question directed to her, Annie went blank.

Stella glanced at her. "It's yours. What do you want to happen?"

Annie considered this a moment. Honestly, she had no idea. She still had to sort through the effects of Stella's confession before taking a step forward. And then there was the question of Stella's input. Annie knew she deserved a part in it to make her whole again. "I think you should have a say in this."

"No." Stella stood adamant. "Your grandmother may have created this lovely piece, but ultimately, she left it to you. You must decide."

And that, Annie found, was easier said than done.

～ 19 ～

Marisa cornered Annie the moment Mary Beth let customers back into the store. "Okay, what do I have to do to exhibit the Betsy Original?"

"Honestly, I haven't decided what to do with the piece." So much had changed in the hour. Now Annie had Stella to consider.

"Well, you have an offer. I'd like to show it," Marisa pressed.

Annie glanced across the room to the cross-stitch, seeing it with a different attitude. Knowing that Stella was the young woman in the picture put a whole new slant on things. This was personal, after all, to her grandmother and to Stella. At this point, Annie wasn't sure how to proceed. Figuring out the meaning behind the cross-stitch had consumed so much of her waking hours. Now, she was at a loss at what to do next.

Marisa wandered off, leaving Annie alone. Exhausted by the emotional rollercoaster she'd just ridden, she didn't think she had the energy to drive home, but needed to escape for a while and think about all the events of the day. She grabbed her purse and car keys when Ian stopped her at the door.

"Looks like you're ready to bolt."

"Is it that obvious?"

"Pretty much." His brows angled with concern. "You okay?"

"I will be eventually."

"Why is that?"

"I learned that Stella is the Lady in the piece."

Ian looked at her with surprise. "I didn't see that coming."

"No one did."

"Then I guess telling you that the Robert's property originally belonged to Stella's family won't come as a surprise."

"If you'd told me yesterday, yes. Not now."

He glanced over at Stella, silently observing her. Then he turned back and said, "Well, you solved the mystery. Does that mean you're leaving town?"

Her stomach rolled as she considered that thought. Did she want to leave? She'd spent another awesome summer here in her old stomping grounds. The mystery, her excuse not to leave, had been solved. The work at Grey Gables was almost finished. Summer would soon turn into fall. Was there anything to keep her here?

She watched her new friends, laughing and surrounding Stella in friendship. She thought about how much she'd enjoyed spending time with them. She knew she wanted to get to know them better. And she still had Grey Gables to consider. And then there was LeeAnn and the grandkids. What about them?

"Annie?" Ian asked patiently.

"I'm afraid I don't have an answer."

"You don't have to decide right this minute, do you?"

She smiled warmly at him. "Truth be told, no, there's no real rush."

Apparently satisfied by her answer, Ian shoved his hands in his pants pockets. "I'm glad, because you've become a real part of this community, whether you realize it or not."

"High praise, coming from the mayor himself."

He grinned. "I'm all about town promotion." With that, he dipped his head in goodbye, exiting the store—his welcome words echoing in Annie's ears.

*   *   *   *

The next morning Annie hurried about, dressing for the day and feeding Boots. She'd called an emergency meeting of the Hook and Needle Club, and she needed to get there on time. Today, along with her crochet, she had two special items with her. She couldn't wait to get downtown.

After a sleepless night, Annie had made her decisions. The club members had let her be, sensing she needed time to think things through, and she was grateful for that. What she didn't need was their ever ready opinions and suggestions. They meant well, these good friends of hers, ready to help her ... if, and when, she asked. Earlier that morning, she'd spoken to LeeAnn, who, surprisingly, agreed with her decisions. One hurdle, probably the toughest, was over.

When she arrived at A Stitch in Time, she peeked through the window to see the women assembled, seated in their usual spots. Annie grinned. It would be a rare day that she ever beat these women to a meeting again.

"Good morning," she sang out as she entered the shop.

"Someone's in a good mood," Mary Beth said in greeting.

"You know what? I am in a good mood. I spoke to my

daughter earlier—always a good way to start the day."

"Have you decided about the Lady?" Peggy asked, coming right to the point.

"I have." Annie took a seat. "I called Marisa before I came over. I told her my decision depends on Stella."

Stella dropped her sweater and needles onto her lap. "Oh, Annie. I stopped your grandmother's work from being showcased years ago. Don't let me be the reason you hesitate now."

"Good, because I hoped you'd say that. Marisa and I came to an agreement."

"Meaning what?" Alice asked.

"Here's the deal. I've offered to let Marisa show it in Boston for the length of the Celebrate Americana exhibit. That way Betsy's work is finally showcased in a museum. But then it comes back home to Stony Point where it belongs." She turned to Stella. "I'd be honored if you would then give it a permanent showcase at your new cultural center."

Stella's eyes grew wide. "I'd hoped so much ... but didn't want to ask."

"I think my grandmother would be pleased."

"Then, of course." Stella's voice cracked, "the Lady will always have a home."

Annie smiled, happy that her part in the mystery had been solved. While the women chatted on about the exhibit, Annie pulled out the letter she'd originally found, along with the frame and the cigar box from Gram's bedroom.

"I think you should have these," she told Stella, handing the items to her.

Curious, Stella set the box on her lap and opened the

letter first. Annie watched her read the words and seconds later, as the message touched her, Stella closed her eyes and pressed the stationery to her chest, right over her heart. When she opened them again, she looked directly at Annie. A moist sheen brightened her eyes.

"Was that from Betsy?" Annie asked.

"Yes. She had such beautiful handwriting when we were younger."

Relieved to have that confirmed, she nodded at the box. "Go ahead, open it," Annie urged.

"You want to give an old lady heart failure," Stella teased. With shaking fingers, she lifted the lid of the box. Slowly, with great care, she examined the contents.

Realizing all the women were beyond curious, Annie's heart wrenched as another part of her grandmother's life was about to be revealed. "I figured those things had meaning to you both."

After a long look, Stella removed the silver frame with shaking hands. "I can't remember who snapped that picture. We were down at the docks that day, waiting for her father to finish working. I had a similar picture, but I've misplaced it over the years."

She glanced at Annie, a wealth of regret in her eyes. Knowing Stella's story, Annie imagined Stella had intentionally gotten rid of the photo.

"May I?" Mary Beth asked.

Stella handed her the frame, then set her attention back to the box. With a grin, she removed the candy wrapper and movie tickets. "We always wanted to go to the movies. Betsy found us a ride to Portland and the brand-new cinema. We talked about that film all summer."

Stella set the tickets and wrappers back in the box and removed the hankie, chuckling while doing so. "This was my first attempt at fine stitching. The blue wildflowers were Betsy's favorite. I tried to make my own design, but Betsy was much better at it." She touched the thread with her fingertips. "Now you can see why I stick to knitting."

"It's lovely," Kate told her, sincerity in her voice.

"No, it's not," Stella groaned. "I have no secrets left now."

A smattering of laughter filled the circle.

"You tried, that's all that mattered," Annie reassured her.

Tears threatened again in Stella's eyes. "That's just what Betsy said."

Peggy propped her chin on her hand as she rested her elbow on the arm of the chair. "This has been one amazing summer."

Alice laughed. "You're not kidding."

"There is one more subject we haven't covered," Alice brought up. "Are you going back to Texas, Annie? Or are you staying home in Stony Point?"

It all came down to this, Annie realized. For her and the amazing women she'd met this wonderful summer. The Lady in the Attic may have been the conduit that had given Annie back the purpose and joy in her life, but the new friendships she'd made stitched her tattered heart together along the journey.

"I'm not leaving Grey Gables, or y'all, yet," she announced, her heart full and happy. "Besides, if I know my grandmother, I'm sure she's left a few more mysteries for us to solve."

Diagonal Squares Shawl

Design by Rena V. Stevens

Crochet Pattern

Skill Level

◼◼◻◻ **EASY**

Finished Measurements

80 inches wide x 40 inches long, excluding Fringe

Materials

- Premier Yarns Luna light (DK) weight acrylic yarn (3½ oz/ 273 yds/100g per skein):
  4 skeins #1072-18 Uranus
- Size G/6/4mm crochet hook or size needed to obtain gauge
- Stitch markers

Gauge

1 square = 1¼ inches; 2 rows = 3 inches

Pattern Notes

Shawl is worked in one piece from right to left edge.

When fastening off at ends of rows, leave 7-inch tails to incorporate into Fringe.

Join with slip stitch as indicated unless otherwise stated.

Yarn ends at beginning of rows can be worked over in Edging.

To watch a video tutorial for this project, sign in to your account at www.AnniesFiction.com.
Click on My Series in the left-hand column, then select Annie's Attic Mysteries, Special Edition.

Special Stitch

Square: Ch 4, 4 tr around indicated tr.

Shawl

Body

Note: First row will seem loose until next row is worked. Beg of row 1 is top edge of Shawl.

Row 1 (RS): Ch 217 loosely, sc in 2nd ch from hook, ch 1, sk next 4 chs, *tr in next ch, **square** *(see Special Stitch)* around last tr made**, sk next 5 chs; rep from * across, ending last rep at **, ch 1, **fasten off** *(see Pattern Notes)*, do not turn. *(36 squares)*

Row 2 (RS): Join *(see Pattern Notes)* in 4th ch of first square, ch 4, *tr in 4th ch of next square, square around last tr made, rep from * across, ch 1, fasten off, do not turn. *(35 squares)*

Row 3–36: Rep row 2. *(1 square at end of last row)*

Left Side Chain

Row 1: With RS facing, join in 4th ch of last square of last row, working along ends of rows, ch 3, sc in 2nd ch from hook *(sk ch counts as ch-1 sp)*, ch 4, sk 3 tr of same square, sc in last tr of same square, *ch 6, sk next ch-4 and 3 tr of next square, sc in last tr of same square, rep from * across edge, ch 1, fasten off. *(35 ch-6 sps, 1 ch-4 sp)*

Sc Edging

Rnd 1: With RS facing, join in first sc of row 1 of Body, (ch 1, sc, ch 1, 2 sc) in same sc, place marker in last ch-1 sp made as corner, working along ends of rows on right side, sc in next ch-1 sp, **working over yarn ends** *(see Pattern Notes)*, *sc in top of next

worked-around tr, 2 sc around ch-4 of same square, sc in 4th ch of same ch-4**, 4 sc around next ch-4 sp, rep from * across, ending last rep at ** , sc in ch-1 sp from beg of Left Side Chain, (2 sc, ch 1, 2 sc) in next sc, place marker in last ch-1 made as corner, without working over yarn ends, 3 sc in next ch sp, [sc in next sc, 4 sc in next ch sp] across to last sc on same edge, 3 sc in next sc *(corner)*, working in last square of row 1 of Body, sc in top of last tr and 2 sc around post of same tr, working in opposite side of foundation chs, 3 sc in first foundation ch *(corner)*, [4 sc around next 5 unworked chs, sc in next worked ch] across, ending with 3 sc around last 4 unworked chs, join in beg ch-1, fasten off. *(290 sc between 2 marked ch sps)*

Top Edging

Row 1 (WS): With WS facing, on top edge, join in first sc after marked corner, (ch 3, 2 dc) in same sc, 2 dc in next sc, [ch 2, sk next 2 sc, dc in each of next 2 sc] across to last 4 sc before next marker, ch 2, sk next 2 sc, 2 dc in next sc, 3 dc in last sc, turn. *(73 ch sps)*

Row 2 (RS): Ch 1, sc in each of first 5 dc, [2 sc in next ch sp, sc in next 2 dc] across, ending with sc in last 4 dc, sc in top of beg ch-3, fasten off.

Fringe

Cut 13-inch strands of yarn. Use 4 or 5 strands including tails in each Fringe. For each Fringe, fold 4- or 5-strand hank in half. Insert hook from RS in indicated sp or st, pull folded end through, catching beg and end tails in Fringe, pull ends through fold, pull ends to tighten knot. On left edge, place Fringe in top corner of Top Edging and Fringe in corner of sc Edging. Incorporating yarn ends, place Fringe in first sc made in each ch sp and in bottom corner of shawl.

Rep for right edge. ●

CROCHET STANDARD ABBREVIATIONS

beg	begin/begins/beginning
bpdc	back post double crochet
bpsc	back post single crochet
bptr	back post treble crochet
CC	contrasting color
ch(s)	chain(s)
ch-	refers to chain or space previously made (i.e., ch-1 space)
ch sp(s)	chain space(s)
cl(s)	cluster(s)
cm	centimeter(s)
dc	double crochet (singular/plural)
dc dec	double crochet 2 or more stitches together, as indicated
dec	decrease/decreases/decreasing
dtr	double treble crochet
ext	extended
fpdc	front post double crochet
fpsc	front post single crochet
fptr	front post treble crochet
g	gram(s)
hdc	half double crochet
hdc dec	half double crochet 2 or more stitches together, as indicated

inc	increase/increases/increasing
lp(s)	loop(s)
MC	main color
mm	millimeter(s)
oz	ounce(s)
pc	popcorn(s)
rem	remain/remains/remaining
rep(s)	repeat(s)
rnd(s)	round(s)
RS	right side
sc	single crochet
sc dec	single crochet 2 or more stitches together, as indicated
sk	skip/skipped/skipping
sl st(s)	slip stitch(es)
sp(s)	space(s)/spaced
st(s)	stitch(es)
tog	together
tr	treble crochet
trtr	triple treble
WS	wrong side
yd(s)	yard(s)
yo	yarn over

Up to this point, we've been doing all the writing. Now it's *your* turn!

Tell us what you think about this book, the characters, the bad guy, or anything else you'd like to share with us about this series. We can't wait to hear from *you*!

Log on to give us your feedback at:
https://www.surveymonkey.com/r/AnniesAttic

Annie's® FICTION